ELARA AND
THE
DOOR OF DAWN

A Tale of Light and Courage

by Rahul PR

Dedication

To my family and friends, whose unwavering love and belief in me lit the path through my own forests of doubt. To the dreamers who see magic in the ordinary, and to those who dare to cross their own hidden doors in search of something greater. This story is for you, and for the spark of courage that lives in us all.

— Rahul PR

Author's Note

Dear Reader,

When I first imagined "Elara and the Door of Dawn", I was sitting under a starlit sky in my hometown, captivated by the idea of a hidden world just beyond our own—a place where ordinary people could find extraordinary courage. Elara's story grew from that spark, a tale of a young woman from a quiet village who discovers her strength in the face of magic, danger, and doubt. Her journey through Aurora mirrors the moments in our lives when we must step into the unknown, trusting in our hearts and the bonds we forge along the way.

Writing this story has been a labor of love, inspired by my own family's stories of resilience and the timeless wonder of folklore. Elara's courage, Kael's mischief, and Alaric's redemption reflect the qualities I admire in those around me—qualities I hope you'll find in yourself as you turn these pages. The themes of identity, courage, and empathy are woven into every chapter, a reminder that even the smallest light can spark a dawn.

I'm thrilled to share Elara's adventure with you, and I hope it leaves you dreaming of hidden doors and the magic within. As you read, I invite you to join me on Facebook, where I've created a video to bring Aurora's world to life. Watch it, share your thoughts, and let me know—would you cross the door? Your support means the world to me and to this story.

Thank you for stepping into Elara's journey. May you find your own light, wherever your path leads.

With gratitude,
Rahul PR

ELARA AND THE DOOR OF DAWN
Copyright © 2025 by Rahul PR
All rights reserved.

DISCLAIMER

This novel explores themes of grief, guilt, spiritual awakening, and emotional trauma from a faith-based perspective. While rooted in Islamic values, the story is not intended to serve as religious authority or scholarly interpretation.

Readers experiencing grief, mental health challenges, or spiritual crises are encouraged to seek guidance from qualified professionals, scholars, or counselors.

The purpose of this work is to inspire, not to instruct. May it serve as a mirror, not a map.

Table of Contents

Introduction

In the quiet village of Briarwood, where golden fields whispered secrets to the wind and the stars burned bright above, a girl named Elara dreamed of worlds beyond the plow and hearth. Her heart, restless as a river, yearned for the tales her father spun by firelight—stories of a hidden door in Brackenwood Forest, a gateway to Aurora, a realm of twilight skies and rivers that flowed with light. To the villagers, these were mere fancies, bedtime yarns to soothe a child's wonder. But to Elara, they were a call, a promise of something greater waiting just beyond the trees.

As autumn painted the fields in hues of amber and crimson, Elara's life was one of simple rhythms— tending crops with her father, learning the healer's art from her mother. Yet, beneath her steady hands and quiet smile, a spark flickered, a longing for purpose that no harvest could fulfill. When a strange stone slab, etched with glowing runes, surfaced in their field, it was as if fate itself had whispered her name. The map, ancient and alive, pointed to the forest, to the door of legend, and to a destiny she could no longer ignore.Unbeknownst to Elara, Aurora was a land in peril, its magic fading under the grip of a sorceress whose shadow threatened to consume all light. A prophecy spoke of a dawnbringer, a mortal with a heart pure and brave, who would cross the threshold to restore balance.

As Elara stepped into Brackenwood, clutching the map and her courage, she was unaware that her journey would test her soul, forge unbreakable bonds, and awaken a strength she never knew she possessed. This is the tale of Elara, a farmer's daughter turned hero, whose quest to save a dying realm would light the dawn for two worlds—and forever change her own.

Chapter 1:

The Restless Heart

The plow bit into the earth, and Elara pushed it forward with a grunt, her hands calloused against the worn wooden handles. The sun hung high over Briarwood, casting a golden glow across the endless fields of wheat that swayed like a gentle sea. Sweat beaded on her brow, and the earthy scent of freshly turned soil filled her lungs. It was a smell she'd known all her eighteen years, as familiar as her own heartbeat, yet today it felt suffocating. Her mind wasn't here, tethered to the plow and the predictable rhythm of village life. No, she was far away, scaling the jagged peaks of the Silver Mountains, her sword flashing as she faced a dragon with scales like molten rubies.

"Elara!" Her father's voice sliced through her reverie, sharp but not unkind. "You're veering off again."

She blinked, reality snapping back into focus. The plow had strayed, carving a crooked furrow through the field. "Sorry, Papa," she mumbled, correcting her course with a quick tug. The wheat rustled in the breeze, whispering secrets she couldn't quite hear.

Her father, Thom, stood a few paces away, his broad shoulders hunched from years of labor. His face was weathered, etched with lines that told stories of seasons endured, but his hazel eyes—mirrors of her own—held a warmth that softened his stern tone. "Where do you go when you drift off like that?" he asked, wiping his hands on his patched trousers.

Elara hesitated, a sheepish smile tugging at her lips. "Today, I was a pirate captain on the Sapphire Isles, chasing treasure through storms and sea monsters."

He chuckled, a low rumble that carried both affection and a trace of sadness. "Ah, my little dreamer. Always somewhere grander than here." He gestured to the fields, the hills rolling gently in the distance. "But there's treasure in this land too, you know. It's steady. Reliable. One day, it'll be yours to tend."

The weight of his words settled on her like a heavy cloak, pressing down on her restless spirit. Hers to tend. A life mapped out in rows of wheat and seasons of toil. She respected her father, loved him fiercely, but the farm was his dream, not hers. Her heart yearned for the tales she devoured by candlelight—stories of heroes, magic, and lands beyond the hills she'd never crossed. "I know, Papa," she said, her voice quieter than she intended. "It's just… don't you ever wonder what's out there?"

Thom followed her gaze to the horizon, where the golden fields met the shadowy edge of Brackenwood Forest. The trees stood tall and tangled, their dark branches clawing at the sky, a forbidden boundary she'd been warned against since childhood. "Out there?" he said, his tone shifting to something cautious. "Nothing good, Elara. That forest is no place for us."

"Why not?" she pressed, though she'd heard the warnings a hundred times—wild animals, treacherous paths, tales of those who ventured in and never returned.

He sighed, sitting on a weathered log at the field's edge and motioning for her to join him. She set the plow aside and sat, the flask of water he offered cool against her parched throat. "It's dangerous," he began, "and not just because of the wolves or the cliffs. There's an old story—a legend, really—about a door deep in Brackenwood. A magical door, they say, that leads to another world."

Elara's heart quickened, her earlier daydreams paling in comparison. "Another world? What kind?"

Thom shrugged, a faint smile playing on his lips as if indulging a child. "A place called Aurora, or so the tale goes. A realm of wonder and peril, where magic flows like rivers and the sky burns twilight all day long. They say it was crafted by ancient mages, sealed after some great war, and only the worthy can find it. But it's just a story to keep young ones from wandering off."

Her mind raced, painting pictures of glowing rivers and endless dusk. "Has anyone ever looked for it?"

His expression darkened, and he leaned closer, voice low. "No one with sense. And you'd do well to promise me you'll never try, Elara. That forest isn't for dreams—it's for nightmares."

"I promise, Papa," she said, the words slipping out as duty demanded. But inside, a spark flared, wild and defiant. How could she promise to ignore the call of something so extraordinary?

The afternoon sun dipped lower as Elara followed her mother, Mara, into the village clinic, a squat building of stone and timber nestled near Briarwood's heart. The air inside carried the sharp tang of herbs and antiseptic, a scent that spoke of healing and her mother's steady hands. Shelves lined the walls, brimming with jars of dried leaves and salves, while a cot held their patient: Old Man Cedric, his gnarled hands resting on a cane.

"Hold this steady, Elara," Mara instructed, her nimble fingers applying a salve to Cedric's arthritic joints. Her mother's dark hair was streaked with silver, pulled back in a practical braid, and her calm efficiency was a balm to the village's ailments.

Elara pressed the bandage in place, but her thoughts drifted back to the forest, to the legend her father had dangled before her like a forbidden fruit. Another world, just beyond the trees. It was intoxicating, a whisper of possibility she couldn't shake.

"Elara, are you listening?" Mara's voice pulled her back, gentle but firm.

"Yes, Mama. Sorry." She forced a smile, adjusting the bandage.

Mara sighed, her brown eyes searching her daughter's face. "You've been distracted all day. What's on your mind?"

"Just… stories," Elara admitted. "Places beyond Briarwood."

Her mother's smile was soft, understanding. "It's natural to wonder, but our place is here, helping our people. There's honor in that."

"I know," Elara said, though the words rang hollow. She wanted to help, to ease pain as her mother did, but she also wanted to chase the horizon, to unravel mysteries.

Cedric cleared his throat, his voice raspy but warm. "Thank you, Healer Mara. Your touch is a blessing." His gaze shifted to Elara, twinkling with mischief. "And you, lass—what's this I hear about stories?"

"You've been places, haven't you?" she asked, seizing the chance. "What's it like out there?"

The old man's face lit up, wrinkles deepening with memory. "Vast and wild. I've seen cities carved from gold, forests where the trees hum with life, oceans that stretch to the stars. Adventure's a heady thing, girl."

Elara leaned closer, eyes wide. "That sounds incredible. I'd give anything to see it."

Cedric's smile faded, his tone sobering. "But it's not all glory. There's danger—bandits, storms, beasts that hunt in the night. Lost good friends to those perils. Came back with scars and a limp to prove it."

Her excitement dimmed, a shadow of doubt creeping in. "But you don't regret it, do you?"

He paused, considering. "Regret? No. But there's a price, lass. Sometimes, I wonder if it was worth it."

Mara shot him a pointed look. "Don't fill her head with such notions, Cedric."

Elara nodded absently, but Cedric's words lingered, a tangle of warning and allure. Was the price of adventure too steep? Yet even as she questioned it, a quiet voice inside her insisted she had to know for herself.

That evening, the family gathered around their sturdy oak table, a simple meal of vegetable stew and crusty bread steaming before them. The cottage was cozy, its walls adorned with woven tapestries and shelves of Mara's herbs. A fire crackled in the hearth, casting flickering shadows across the room.

Elara picked at her stew, her mind still buzzing from the day. Finally, she couldn't hold back. "Papa, about that legend you mentioned—the door in the forest. Is there more to it?"

Thom raised an eyebrow, spoon pausing midair. "Why the interest, Elara?"

"It's just... I've never heard it before. It's fascinating."

He leaned back, thoughtful, as Mara watched them both with a hint of concern. "It's an old tale," he said, "passed down through generations. They say the door was forged by mages centuries ago, a gateway to Aurora—a land of magic and twilight. It was sealed after a war tore through both worlds, and only someone with a pure heart and a brave spirit can open it again."

Elara's pulse quickened. "Has anyone from Briarwood ever tried?"

Mara interjected, her voice firm. "Of course not. It's a story, nothing more. Besides, the forest is too dangerous."

Thom nodded, but there was a flicker in his eyes—a glimmer of wonder, perhaps, or memory. "Your mother's right. It's best left alone."

Elara pressed her lips together, unconvinced. The way her father spoke, there was something alive in the tale, something that begged to be explored.

Sleep eluded her that night. Elara lay in her narrow bed, the patchwork quilt pulled to her chin, staring at the ceiling beams. Moonlight spilled through the window, painting the floor in silver stripes. The tales of the day swirled in her mind—her father's legend, Cedric's warnings, the glow she'd imagined in the forest during dinner, though she hadn't dared mention it.

Slipping from beneath the covers, she padded to the window, her nightgown brushing the wooden floor. The village lay still, thatched roofs gleaming under the moon, but beyond the houses, Brackenwood loomed, its dark silhouette both menacing and magnetic. As she stared, she thought she saw it again—a faint shimmer deep within the trees, like a lantern's flicker. She rubbed her eyes, and it vanished. A trick of the light, perhaps, or her restless imagination?

Her heart thudded. Maybe it was a sign, a call she couldn't ignore. She didn't know what was true, but she knew she couldn't stay content with unanswered questions. Tomorrow, she'd press her father for more, maybe even search the village hall's dusty records for clues about the legend. Whatever it took, she'd uncover the truth.

With that resolve, she climbed back into bed, her mind alight with possibilities. She drifted into a fitful sleep, unaware that fate was already stirring, that the next day's labor would unearth more than soil—it would set her on a path toward destiny.

Chapter 2:

The Hidden Map

The sun hung low in the sky, casting a warm, golden hue over the fields of Briarwood. The air was crisp with the scent of autumn, and the distant chirping of birds mingled with the rhythmic scrape of the plow cutting through the earth. Elara pushed the heavy tool forward, her hands gripping the worn wooden handles as she followed her father, Thom, through the rows of soil. The work was monotonous, but it gave her mind space to wander—back to the stories she'd read by candlelight, to the legends her father had shared just the day before.

"Elara, keep the lines straight," Thom called over his shoulder, his voice steady but kind. "We need even rows for the seeds."

"Yes, Papa," she replied, snapping her focus back to the task. She adjusted her grip and guided the plow with more care, though her thoughts still drifted. The legend of the door in Brackenwood Forest lingered in her mind like a half-remembered dream. Another world, just beyond the trees. It seemed impossible, yet the idea tugged at her, as if daring her to believe.

They worked in companionable silence for a while, the only sounds the crunch of soil and the occasional grunt of effort. But then, without warning, Elara's plow struck something hard, jerking her to a stop. She stumbled forward, catching herself on the handles.

"Ow!" she exclaimed, wincing as the impact reverberated through her arms.

Thom turned, concern creasing his brow. "What is it?"

"I think it's a rock," Elara said, stepping back to inspect the ground. She knelt beside the plow, brushing away loose dirt with her hands. But as the soil fell away, she realized it wasn't just a rock—it was a flat, rectangular slab of stone, its surface etched with intricate carvings.

Thom crouched beside her, his eyes narrowing as he examined the slab. "That's no ordinary stone," he muttered, running a finger over the weathered symbols. "Looks like some kind of old marking."

Elara leaned closer, her heart quickening. The carvings were unlike anything she'd seen before—swirling patterns that might have been stars, a winding line that could be a river, and in the center, the distinct outline of a door. Her breath caught. A door. Just like the one from the legend.

"Papa, look at this," she said, pointing to the door symbol. "It's like the story you told me—about the door in the forest."

Thom chuckled, though there was a hint of unease in his eyes. "It's probably just an old relic, Elara. Nothing more. Let's move it out of the way so we can finish the field."

But Elara couldn't tear her gaze from the slab. The symbols seemed to beckon her, whispering secrets she couldn't quite hear. "Can I keep it?" she asked, her voice barely above a whisper. "Maybe it's important."

Thom sighed, wiping his hands on his trousers. "If it'll make you happy, go ahead. But don't go spinning tales in your head about treasure maps or hidden doors. We've got real work to do."

Elara nodded, though her pulse raced with excitement. She carefully lifted the slab—it was heavier than it looked—and set it aside, leaning it against a nearby fence post. As she returned to the plow, her mind buzzed with possibilities. What if it "was" a map? What if it led to the door her father had spoken of?

The rest of the afternoon passed in a blur. Elara's body moved through the motions of plowing, but her thoughts were elsewhere, tangled in visions of glowing rivers and twilight skies. By the time the sun dipped below the horizon, casting long shadows across the fields, she was eager to retreat to the privacy of her room.

That evening, after a quiet dinner with her parents, Elara slipped away to her small bedroom at the back of the cottage. The stone slab lay on her desk, illuminated by the soft glow of a single candle. She had smuggled it inside under her cloak, not wanting to draw her parents' attention. Now, alone at last, she could study it properly.

She sat down, her fingers tracing the carvings with reverence. The symbols were intricate, almost hypnotic in their design. There were clusters of stars arranged in unfamiliar constellations, a serpentine line that might be a path or a river, and delicate runes she couldn't decipher. But it was the door that held her gaze—a tall, arched shape with what looked like a keyhole at its center. Surrounding it were smaller symbols, perhaps clues or warnings.

Elara's heart thudded in her chest. This had to be connected to the legend. It was too much of a coincidence otherwise. She fetched a piece of parchment and a quill, intending to copy the map for further study. As she began to trace the lines, a strange sensation washed over her—a faint tingling in her fingertips, as if the stone hummed with a quiet energy.

She paused, holding her breath. For a fleeting moment, the symbols seemed to shimmer, glowing with a soft, ethereal light. Elara gasped and jerked her hand back. The glow vanished as quickly as it had appeared, leaving the map looking ordinary once more.

Was she imagining things? She rubbed her eyes and leaned closer, but the stone remained still, its secrets locked away. Perhaps it was just a trick of the candlelight, or her own wishful thinking. Yet deep down, she knew there was more to it. The map felt "alive", as if it were calling to her.

A soft knock on the door startled her. "Elara? Are you coming to help with the dishes?" her mother's voice called from the hallway.

Elara quickly covered the slab with a cloth. "I'll be there in a minute, Mama!" she replied, her voice steady despite the racing of her heart.

She couldn't let her parents know about this—not yet. They would only worry, or worse, forbid her from investigating further. But the map had ignited something within her, a spark of curiosity too bright to ignore. She had to understand what it meant, even if it meant keeping secrets.

The next morning, after helping her mother with the daily chores, Elara made her way to the village library. It was a small, dusty building tucked between the blacksmith's forge and the market square, its shelves crammed with ancient tomes and yellowed scrolls. If there was any place in Briarwood that might hold answers about the map, it was here.

The librarian, Agnes, greeted her with a warm smile. "Good morning, Elara. What brings you here today?"

"I was wondering if you have any books about old maps or legends of the forest," Elara said, trying to sound casual.

Agnes tapped her chin thoughtfully. "Hmm, there might be something in the history section. Follow me."

She led Elara to a dimly lit corner of the library, where several leather-bound books were stacked haphazardly on a shelf. "These are about the history of Briarwood and the surrounding areas," Agnes explained. "Perhaps you'll find what you're looking for."

Elara thanked her and began sifting through the titles. One book caught her eye: "Tales of Brackenwood". Its cover was worn, the pages brittle with age. She carried it to a nearby table and began to read.

The book was filled with stories of the forest—tales of mythical creatures, lost travelers, and ancient magic. One chapter, in particular, made her pulse quicken. It spoke of a hidden door deep within Brackenwood, a gateway to another realm called Aurora. According to the legend, the door was sealed centuries ago after a great war, and only those with a pure heart could find it and pass through.

Elara's breath caught in her throat. This was it—the same story her father had told her, but with more detail. The book described Aurora as a land of eternal twilight, where rivers flowed with light and the air hummed with magic. It was said to be a place of both wonder and peril, guarded by ancient spells.

But as she read on, her excitement dimmed. The book offered no maps, no directions to the door. It was as if the legend was meant to remain just that—a story, not a guide.

Disappointed, Elara closed the book and returned it to the shelf. As she turned to leave, Agnes's voice stopped her. "Did you find what you were looking for, dear?"

"Not really," Elara admitted, her shoulders slumping. "I was hoping for something more... specific."

Agnes nodded, her eyes twinkling with a hint of mystery. "Sometimes, the answers we seek aren't found in books, but in our own hearts. Trust your instincts, Elara. They'll guide you where you need to go."

Elara pondered those words as she walked home. Maybe Agnes was right. Perhaps she didn't need a book to tell her what to do. She had the map, and she had her curiosity. That was enough.

That evening, as the sun dipped below the horizon and the sky blazed with hues of orange and pink, Elara sat in her room, the map spread out before her. She had studied it for hours, trying to make sense of the symbols. The winding line, she decided, must be a path through the forest. The stars could be a constellation to navigate by, though she wasn't sure which one. And the door—well, that was the goal.

Her parents were in the kitchen, their voices a soft murmur through the walls. Elara knew they would never approve of her venturing into Brackenwood. It was too dangerous, they would say. But the pull of the map was too strong to resist. She had to know if the legend was true, if there really was a door to another world.

A plan began to form in her mind. She would wait until her parents were asleep, then sneak out with the map. She'd follow the path it showed, deep into the forest, and see where it led. It was reckless, perhaps even foolish, but the thought of staying in Briarwood, forever wondering, was unbearable.

She packed a small bag with essentials—a flask of water, some bread and cheese, a lantern, and a warm cloak. Her heart raced with a mixture of fear and excitement. This was it. Her chance for adventure, for something beyond the ordinary.

As she tucked the map into her bag, she noticed something strange. The symbols seemed to shimmer again, just for a moment, as if responding to her decision. Elara blinked, and the glow faded. She shook her head—surely, it was her imagination. But deep down, she felt a quiet certainty. The map was more than just stone and carvings. It was a key, and she was meant to use it.

Later that night, when the cottage was silent and the only light came from the moon outside her window, Elara crept from her bed. She dressed quickly, pulling on sturdy boots and her cloak, then slung the bag over her shoulder. The map was safely tucked inside, its weight both a comfort and a reminder of the unknown that awaited her.

She tiptoed through the house, careful not to wake her parents. The front door creaked softly as she opened it, and she froze, listening for any sign of movement. When none came, she slipped outside, closing the door behind her.

The village lay still under the silver glow of the moon. The air was cool, carrying the scent of pine and damp earth. Elara took a deep breath, steadying her nerves, then turned toward Brackenwood Forest.

Its dark silhouette loomed ahead, the trees like sentinels guarding ancient secrets.

With each step, her resolve strengthened. She was no longer just a farmer's daughter, tethered to the land. She was an explorer, a seeker of truth. And whatever lay beyond the forest—whether danger or wonder—she was ready to face it.

As she reached the edge of the woods, she paused, glancing back at the sleeping village. For a moment, doubt flickered in her mind. What if she was making a mistake? What if the map led to nothing but disappointment?

But then she thought of the stories, of the door, of Aurora. She thought of the restlessness that had plagued her for so long, the yearning for something more. No, she couldn't turn back now.

With a final, determined breath, Elara stepped into the forest, the map's path unfolding before her like a promise.

Little did she know, this was only the beginning. The true adventure—and the dangers that came with it—awaited just beyond the trees.

Chapter 3:

Forbidden Journey

Elara stood at the threshold of Brackenwood Forest, her heart thumping with a blend of excitement and trepidation. The night was deep, the only light streaming from the moon, filtering through a dense canopy of twisted branches to cast shifting shadows on the ground. She inhaled deeply, the cool, damp air rich with the scent of moss and decaying leaves, steadying her nerves for the journey ahead. In her hands, she clutched a lantern—its warm, flickering glow illuminating the gnarled trees—and the stone slab map she'd uncovered in Chapter 2, its carvings faintly visible. With a final glance back at the distant lights of Briarwood village, she stepped into the forbidden woods, her boots crunching on fallen leaves.

The path was little more than a deer trail, narrow and choked with underbrush. As she ventured deeper, Elara noticed something extraordinary: the winding line etched into the map began to glow faintly, pulsing with a soft, ethereal light. It brightened when she moved in the right direction and dimmed if she veered off course. "Incredible," she whispered, marveling at the map's magic, as if it were alive, urging her toward her destination—the legendary door her father had spoken of in whispered tales.

The forest buzzed with life. Crickets chirped in a relentless chorus, owls hooted from unseen perches, and the occasional rustle of small creatures made her jump. Her imagination conjured phantoms in every shadow, but she steeled herself with a mantra: ""Stay calm. You've faced worse."" Had she, though? In Briarwood, the greatest threats were stubborn mules or sudden storms—nothing like the wild, untamed mystery of Brackenwood.

As she pressed on, the trees grew denser, their branches interlocking like skeletal hands overhead, blocking out much of the moonlight. The path became a tangle of roots and thorns, forcing her to pause often to consult the glowing map. Then, she reached a stretch where the undergrowth thickened into a wall of brambles and vines. Hesitating only a moment, she pushed forward, using her free hand to part the foliage while holding the lantern aloft.

Suddenly, the vines moved. They writhed like living tendrils, snapping at her with startling speed, coiling around her ankles and wrists. Elara gasped, the map slipping from her grasp as she flailed against their tightening grip. Panic clawed at her chest.

"'Plants don't move like this,'" she thought, but in Brackenwood, the impossible seemed ordinary. Her father's warnings echoed in her mind—"'That forest is no place for the living'"—and for a fleeting second, she regretted her defiance.

But surrender wasn't an option. She'd come too far. Gritting her teeth, she fumbled for the small knife tucked in her boot. With careful, desperate slashes, she severed the vines, their ends recoiling as if wounded. Free at last, she stumbled forward, snatching the map from the ground and leaning against a tree to catch her breath. Her pulse raced, her limbs trembled. That had been too close. She resolved to tread more cautiously, the forest's dangers now starkly real.

Regaining her composure, Elara resumed her trek, the map's glow guiding her through the oppressive silence that had settled over the woods. Then, a low growl shattered the stillness, freezing her in place. Her lantern swung as she turned, its light catching two glowing eyes in the darkness. A massive, wolf-like creature emerged—larger than any beast she'd seen, its black fur blending with the night, its bared teeth glinting menacingly.

Her mind raced. Outrunning it was impossible, and her knife felt laughably inadequate against such a foe. Then, she recalled a trick from the adventure tales she'd devoured as a child. Moving slowly to avoid provoking it, she bent down and picked up a fist-sized stone. The creature growled again, stalking closer. With a surge of adrenaline, she hurled the stone as far as she could to her right. It crashed through the underbrush, and the beast's head snapped toward the sound, its ears pricking.

Seizing the moment, Elara darted behind a thick trunk, pressing herself against the bark and holding her breath. She heard the creature sniff the air, then its heavy paws padded away toward the distraction. Counting silently to ten, she peeked out—the path was clear. Exhaling a shaky breath, she hurried onward, her legs unsteady but her resolve hardening. She'd faced danger and survived; she could do this.

After what felt like hours—though the moon's position suggested mere minutes—the trees began to thin, and Elara stepped into a small clearing. At its heart stood a towering oak, ancient and immense, its trunk wider than her cottage back home, its gnarled roots sprawling like veins across the earth. Its branches stretched skyward, a silhouette against the moonlit night. Embedded in the trunk was a door, its weathered wood adorned with intricate carvings that mirrored those on her map.

Elara approached, her eyes wide with awe. The air here felt charged, alive with an unseen energy. She reached out, her fingers brushing the cool, rough surface of the door. A tingle shot up her arm, and a faint hum seemed to rise from the forest itself, as if it recognized her presence. This was it—the door to Aurora, the realm of legend her father had described, the destination that had fueled her restless dreams.

A large keyhole stared back at her, but she had no key. As she traced the carvings, a whisper brushed her mind: "'Only the worthy may pass.'" Her breath caught. Was she worthy? Doubt flickered, but she silenced it. She'd defied her parents, braved snapping vines and a snarling beast, and followed a glowing map to this moment. She had to try.

With a deep breath, she placed both hands on the door and pushed. To her astonishment, the carvings flared with a soft, golden light, and the door quivered beneath her touch. With a low, resonant groan, it swung inward, revealing a shimmering portal. Beyond it lay a glimpse of another world—rivers flowing with liquid light, trees aglow with starry leaves, a sky awash in twilight hues.

Elara stepped back, her gasp swallowed by the night. Aurora. It was real. Her heart soared, a wild mix of triumph and fear pulsing through her. She'd found the door, but what now? The threshold beckoned, promising answers to the yearning that had driven her from Briarwood. Yet, as she stood there, a shadow of doubt lingered. Was she truly ready for what lay ahead?

She glanced back at the dark forest, then squared her shoulders. This was her path, her chance to become more than a restless girl from a quiet village. With the portal's light bathing her face, Elara prepared to step into the unknown.

Chapter 4:

The Door to Aurora

Elara's heart pounded as she pushed against the ancient oak door, its carvings warm beneath her palms. The air crackled, and a pulse of golden light flared from the wood, swallowing her in a rush of warmth and weightlessness. For a breathless moment, she was nowhere—suspended in a void where sound and time ceased. Then, with a soft thud, her boots met solid ground, and the light dissolved, revealing a world that stole her breath.

She stood on a hill overlooking a vast, shimmering expanse. The grass glowed with a faint, silvery luminescence, rippling like a sea under an unseen wind. Rivers of liquid light wove through the landscape, their currents sparkling like molten stars, humming a soft, haunting melody that tugged at her soul. Towering trees, their trunks silver and leaves aglow with hues of amethyst and gold, framed the horizon, their branches swaying as if whispering secrets to one another. Above, a twilight sky stretched endlessly, awash in deep indigo and soft rose, dotted with stars that pulsed like living things.

This was Aurora. Elara's lips parted in a silent gasp, her eyes drinking in the impossible beauty. The tales her father had spun—stories she'd half-believed were mere fancies—paled against this reality. The air tasted sweet, tinged with a faint metallic tang, and it buzzed against her skin, alive with an energy that made her pulse race. She clutched the stone map, its carvings now dim, and took a step forward, her boots sinking into the radiant grass.

But as she moved deeper into the meadow, a shadow crept into her awe. The rivers' glow flickered in places, dimming like a candle starved of air. Some trees stood barren, their leaves brittle and gray, curling like ash. The melody of the rivers carried a discordant note, a faint wail beneath its beauty. The land was sick, its vibrancy fraying at the edges, and the realization settled in Elara's chest like a stone. Aurora was dying.

A sharp rustle snapped her from her thoughts. She spun, her lantern swinging in her grip, its light catching a pair of gleaming eyes in the grass. A creature emerged—small, fox-like, with fur like a sunset, orange and red shimmering as if lit from within. It tilted its head, studying her with unsettling intelligence.

"Well, well," it said, its voice smooth and teasing, like a bard mid-tale. "A mortal in Aurora. Didn't expect you to be so... ordinary."

Elara's jaw dropped. "You talk?"

The creature smirked, revealing sharp, glinting teeth. "Brilliantly, I might add. I'm Kael, guardian of this fading realm. And you are?"

"Elara," she stammered, still reeling. "From Briarwood."

Kael's tail flicked, his eyes narrowing with playful skepticism. "Elara from Briarwood, stumbling through a magical door with a glowing map. Not your average farmer, are you?"

Before she could respond, a heavy tread sounded behind her. A tall figure stepped from the shadows of a gnarled tree, his armor scarred and tarnished, its once-silver sheen dulled by time. His face was rugged, a jagged scar slicing across one cheek, and his gray eyes held a weariness that made Elara's heart ache. He carried a sword at his hip, its hilt worn but steady in his grip.

"This is Ser Alaric," Kael said, bounding onto a nearby rock for a better view. "Exiled knight, brooding hero, and my reluctant partner in keeping Aurora from collapsing."

Alaric's gaze locked onto Elara, sharp and assessing. "You're the one the prophecy spoke of," he said, his voice low, like gravel underfoot. "The dawnbringer."

Elara's stomach twisted. "Prophecy? Dawnbringer? You've got the wrong person. I'm just—"

"The door opened for you," Alaric cut in, his tone unyielding. "That's no small thing. Only the worthy can pass."

Kael hopped down, circling her with a grin. "He's right, you know. That map you're clutching? It's no ordinary rock. It chose you, led you here. And trust me, Aurora doesn't let just anyone waltz in."

Elara's fingers tightened around the map, its weight grounding her amidst the surreal. "Why me? What's happening to this place?"

Kael's grin faded, his ears flattening. "Aurora's under a curse. Our ruler, Princess Liora, is trapped— her spirit locked in a crystal orb by Morgath, a sorceress with a knack for ruining everything.

Morgath's draining the realm's magic, and without Liora's light, the land's fading fast."

Elara glanced at the withered trees, the faltering rivers. "That's why it feels… broken."

"Exactly," Alaric said, stepping closer. "The rivers dim, the trees weaken, and the twilight grows darker each day. If we don't stop Morgath, Aurora will crumble—and its magic may bleed into your world."

The thought sent a chill through her. Briarwood, her parents, the quiet fields—could they be touched by this darkness? She swallowed, her throat dry. "What do I have to do?"

Kael's eyes gleamed with approval. "Find the Heart of Radiance, a crystal that holds the power to break Morgath's curse and free Liora. It's hidden beyond the Three Realms—nasty places full of trials that test even the bravest souls."

"Trials?" Elara's voice wavered, but she forced it steady. "What kind?"

"The kind that break you if you're not careful," Alaric said, his scar seeming to deepen in the

45

twilight. "Morgath's power grows stronger, and her spies are everywhere. We can't linger here."

Elara's mind spun. She was no hero, no mage. She was a farmer's daughter who'd chased a legend on a whim. But the pain in Alaric's eyes, the urgency in Kael's voice, and the dying land around her stirred something deep within. She couldn't walk away— not when she'd felt Aurora's heartbeat, its magic calling to her own restless spirit.

"I'll do it," she said, her voice firm despite the tremor in her hands. "I'll help you find the Heart."

Kael's grin returned, sharp and infectious. "That's the spirit, dawnbringer! Stick with us, and you might just survive."

Alaric's expression softened, just a fraction. "We head to Lumina, a village still holding out against Morgath's shadow. We'll gather supplies and allies there."

Elara nodded, falling into step beside them as they moved toward a path winding through the glowing meadow. The grass brushed her legs, its light dimming slightly, as if mourning their departure. Kael bounded ahead, his tail a flicker of fire in the dusk, while Alaric's steady presence anchored her.

As they neared the forest's edge, a prickle of unease crawled up Elara's spine. She paused, glancing back. In the distance, where the door had stood, a shadow moved—a cloaked figure, its form indistinct but its presence heavy with malice. Her breath hitched. "There's someone there," she whispered, pointing.

Kael's ears twitched, and Alaric's hand flew to his sword. They followed her gaze, but the figure melted into the trees, leaving only the rustle of leaves in its wake.

"Morgath's eyes," Alaric growled, his grip tightening on his hilt. "She knows you're here."

Elara's heart raced, the weight of their mission crashing down. She was in a world of magic and danger, hunted by a sorceress who could shatter her with a thought. Yet, as she clutched the map and felt the hum of Aurora's fading magic, a spark of defiance flared within her. She wasn't just Elara from Briarwood anymore. She was something more—something this realm needed.

As they vanished into the forest, the shadow lingered, its whisper carried on the wind: "The dawnbringer walks." The words slithered through the trees, a promise of the battles to come.

Chapter 5:

Strangers in a Strange Land

Elara's boots sank into the glowing grass of Aurora as she followed Kael and Ser Alaric along a winding path through the meadow. The twilight sky cast an otherworldly glow, bathing the trio in hues of violet and gold. The air hummed with a faint, restless energy, like a song caught in a minor key. Around her, the landscape of Aurora unfolded in breathtaking detail—trees with leaves like stained glass, rivers of liquid light that rippled with a mournful melody, and flowers that pulsed faintly, as if struggling to hold their radiance. Yet, the signs of decay were unmistakable: patches of grass lay dull and brittle, and some trees sagged, their branches bare and skeletal.

Kael bounded ahead, his fox-like form a flicker of orange in the dusk, his tail swishing with restless energy. "Keep up, dawnbringer!" he called, his voice laced with teasing mischief. "We don't have all eternity—though it might feel like it in this endless twilight."

Elara quickened her pace, clutching the stone map in her bag. Its carvings had dimmed since she crossed the door, but its weight reassured her, a tether to the world she'd left behind. "I'm trying," she shot back, a small smile tugging at her lips despite the unease gnawing at her. Kael's levity was a spark in the gloom, but Ser Alaric's silence was a heavy counterweight.

The knight walked beside her, his scarred armor clinking softly with each step. His face was a mask of stoic resolve, but his gray eyes flickered with something deeper—grief, perhaps, or guilt. He hadn't spoken since warning her of Morgath's spies, and his brooding presence made Elara feel both safe and unsettled.

"Where exactly is Lumina?" she asked, breaking the silence. "And why is it safe?"

Alaric's gaze remained fixed on the path ahead. "Lumina is a village on the edge of the Starlit Vale, shielded by old wards. Morgath's influence hasn't fully reached it—yet. We'll find shelter and supplies there, maybe even allies."

"Allies?" Elara echoed, her brow furrowing. "Are there others fighting against her?"

Kael snorted, leaping onto a low branch to peer down at her. "Fighting? Most of Aurora's folk are too scared to sneeze without Morgath's permission. But there are a few brave—or foolish—souls in Lumina who might join us. Assuming they don't run screaming at the sight of a mortal."

Elara's stomach twisted. "They don't like humans?"

"Not exactly," Kael said, his grin sharp. "They just don't trust outsiders. Last time a mortal wandered through, things got… messy. Long story, bad ending."

Alaric shot Kael a warning glance. "Enough. She doesn't need more doubts."

Elara appreciated the knight's defense, but Kael's words stung. She was an outsider here, a girl from Briarwood with no magic, no training, only a map and a prophecy she didn't fully believe. "What happened to the last mortal?" she asked, unable to resist.

Kael's ears flicked, and he dropped back to the ground, padding beside her. "Let's just say they thought they could outsmart Morgath. Spoiler: they couldn't. But you? You've got us, so you're already ahead."

His attempt at reassurance didn't quite land, but Elara forced a nod. "Right. Lucky me."

As they walked, the path dipped into a grove where the trees grew denser, their glowing leaves casting dappled light across the ground. The air grew cooler, and the rivers' melody faded, replaced by a faint rustling that set Elara's nerves on edge. She glanced over her shoulder, half-expecting to see the shadowy figure from the meadow, but the path behind was empty.

"Tell me more about Morgath," she said, her voice low. "What does she want?"

Alaric's jaw tightened, and for a moment, she thought he wouldn't answer. Then he spoke, his words clipped. "Power. Always power. Morgath was once Liora's advisor, gifted with magic that rivaled the princess's. But she craved more—control over Aurora's essence, its very lifeblood. When Liora refused her demands, Morgath turned on her, cursing her into the orb and siphoning the realm's magic for herself."

Elara's heart sank. "And Liora? What's she like?"

Kael's eyes softened, a rare glimpse of sincerity. "Liora was… is… Aurora's heart. Her light kept the rivers flowing, the trees singing. She's kind, fierce, and stubborn as a storm. Without her, this place is just a shadow of itself."

The weight of their words pressed on Elara. A sorceress bent on domination, a trapped princess, a dying world—and somehow, "she" was supposed to fix it. Doubt gnawed at her, but she pushed it down, focusing on the path ahead.

The grove opened into a clearing where a small bridge arched over a stream of liquid light. Its surface shimmered, but dark patches marred its glow, like ink spilled in water. Elara paused, crouching to peer into the stream. Her reflection stared back, distorted by the flickering light, her hazel eyes wide with wonder and fear.

"Careful," Alaric warned, his voice sharp. "The rivers are tied to Aurora's magic. They're unstable now."

As if in response, the stream rippled violently, and a tendril of light lashed out, grazing Elara's hand. She yelped, stumbling back, her skin stinging as if burned. Kael darted to her side, sniffing her hand. "You'll live," he said, though his tone held a trace of concern. "But let's not poke the dying magic, yeah?"

Elara rubbed her hand, the pain fading but the warning clear. Aurora was as dangerous as it was beautiful. She stood, brushing off her cloak, and followed her companions across the bridge.

As they continued, Kael filled the silence with chatter—tales of Aurora's past, from starlit festivals to battles with shadow-beasts. His stories painted a vibrant world, but they also underscored its fragility. Alaric, meanwhile, remained quiet, his eyes scanning the trees as if expecting an ambush. Elara noticed the way his hand never strayed far from his sword, and it made her own senses sharpen.

They reached a rise overlooking a valley, where the village of Lumina came into view. Nestled among glowing trees, its thatched roofs and stone cottages shimmered with faint wards—barriers of light that pulsed weakly, like a heartbeat struggling to hold steady. Smoke curled from chimneys, and figures moved in the distance, their forms indistinct in the twilight.

"Lumina," Alaric said, his voice softening slightly. "We'll rest here tonight."

Elara nodded, but her attention was drawn to a flicker of movement in the trees to their left. A shadow darted between the trunks, too swift to be natural. Her pulse quickened. "There," she whispered, pointing. "I saw something."

Kael's ears swiveled, and Alaric drew his sword, its blade catching the twilight's glow. They stood still, the air thick with tension. For a moment, nothing happened. Then a low, guttural hiss echoed from the shadows, followed by the snap of a twig.

"Morgath's minions," Alaric growled, stepping in front of Elara. "Kael, scout ahead."

Kael nodded, his playful demeanor gone as he melted into the underbrush, silent as a wraith. Elara's hand tightened on her bag, the map's weight a reminder of why she was here. She wasn't helpless— she'd faced vines and a wolf in Brackenwood—but the thought of Morgath's creatures sent a shiver through her.

A moment later, Kael returned, his fur bristling. "Two shadow-wraiths," he reported, his voice low. "They're circling, likely reporting to Morgath. We need to move—now."

Alaric's eyes narrowed. "To Lumina. The wards will hold them off."

They broke into a run, Elara's heart pounding as she followed. The path sloped downward, the glowing grass blurring beneath her feet. Behind them, the hissing grew louder, accompanied by the rustle of unseen pursuers. Elara risked a glance back, catching a glimpse of dark, formless shapes weaving through the trees, their eyes glowing like embers.

"Faster!" Alaric urged, his armor clanking as he led the way.

They reached the edge of Lumina, where the wards flared briefly, a lattice of light that made the air hum. The hissing stopped abruptly, as if the creatures dared not cross the barrier. Elara stumbled to a halt, gasping for breath, her hands on her knees. Kael panted beside her, his tail flicking nervously, while Alaric stood guard, his sword still drawn.

"They're gone," Kael said, his voice tight. "For now."

Elara straightened, her chest heaving. "What were those things?"

"Shadow-wraiths," Alaric said, sheathing his sword. "Morgath's creations, born from her stolen magic. They're her eyes and claws in the wilds."

Elara's stomach churned. If those were just spies, what else did Morgath command? She looked toward Lumina, its lights a fragile beacon in the twilight. "Will we be safe there?"

"As safe as anywhere in Aurora," Kael replied, his grin returning but strained. "Come on, dawnbringer. Let's see if Lumina's folk think you're worth betting on."

As they approached the village, Elara felt the weight of their stares—figures in doorways, their eyes wary and curious. She was a stranger in a strange land, marked by a prophecy she didn't understand, hunted by a sorceress she'd never met. But as she glanced at Kael's flickering tail and Alaric's steady presence, a spark of resolve ignited within her. She was here, and she would fight—for Aurora, for her home, for the restless heart that had led her to this moment.

Unseen in the shadows beyond the wards, a wraith lingered, its ember-eyes fixed on Elara. It hissed softly, a message sent to its mistress: the dawnbringer was moving, and the hunt was on.

Chapter 6:

The Prophecy Unveiled

The wards of Lumina shimmered as Elara, Kael, and Ser Alaric crossed into the village, their faint glow pulsing like a heartbeat in the endless twilight of Aurora. The air was warmer here, tinged with the scent of blooming nightflowers and woodsmoke, but the hum of magic felt fragile, as if it might unravel at any moment. Elara's boots crunched on the cobblestone path winding through the village, its cottages built of pale stone and woven vines, their roofs aglow with luminescent moss. Figures moved in the shadows—villagers with wary eyes and hushed voices, their gazes lingering on Elara, the outsider.

Kael bounded ahead, his orange fur catching the light like a flame. "Welcome to Lumina, dawnbringer," he said, his voice bright but edged with caution. "Try not to stare too much. These folk aren't used to mortals."

Elara adjusted the strap of her bag, the stone map heavy against her hip. "I'm not staring," she muttered, though her eyes darted to a woman weaving a basket from glowing reeds, her fingers moving with unnatural grace. Everything here felt alive, infused with magic, yet the villagers' faces were drawn, their movements hurried. The curse was palpable, a weight pressing on the land and its people.

Ser Alaric walked beside her, his scarred armor clinking softly. His silence was a steady presence, but Elara caught the tension in his jaw, the way his hand hovered near his sword. "Stay close," he said, his voice low. "Morgath's wraiths won't cross the wards, but her influence creeps even here."

Elara nodded, her pulse quickening at the memory of the shadow-wraiths' ember-eyes. She glanced over her shoulder, half-expecting to see those glowing orbs in the trees beyond the village, but the forest was still, its branches swaying in a breeze she couldn't feel.

They approached a low, domed building at the village's heart, its walls etched with runes that pulsed faintly, like stars struggling to shine. "The Library of Lumina," Kael announced, hopping onto a stone bench. "Old, dusty, and full of secrets. If we're to understand this prophecy nonsense, this is the place."

"Prophecy nonsense?" Elara raised an eyebrow. "I thought you believed I was the dawnbringer."

Kael's grin was sharp. "I believe you're "something", mortal. Whether you're the hero of legend or just lucky, we'll find out soon enough."

Alaric shot him a stern look. "Enough, Kael. She's here, and that's what matters." He pushed open the library's heavy wooden door, its hinges creaking as it swung inward.

Inside, the air was thick with the musty scent of ancient parchment and the faint glow of floating orbs that illuminated towering shelves crammed with scrolls and tomes. The ceiling was a mosaic of stained glass, depicting a radiant figure—perhaps Princess Liora—holding a glowing crystal. Elara's breath caught at the sight, her hand instinctively brushing the map in her bag. Was that crystal the Heart of Radiance?

A figure emerged from the shadows, cloaked in robes of deep indigo. The woman was elderly, her silver hair braided tightly, her eyes milky white yet piercing, as if she saw beyond the physical world. "Welcome, travelers," she said, her voice soft but resonant, like wind through reeds. "I am Sylvara, the Keeper of Lore. I sensed your arrival."

Elara's skin prickled. "You knew we were coming?"

Sylvara's lips curved in a faint smile. "The threads of fate hum when a dawnbringer steps into Aurora. Come, sit. We have much to discuss."

They followed her to a round table carved with runes, its surface littered with open scrolls. Elara sat, her hands clasped tightly to still their trembling. Kael perched on the table's edge, his tail flicking, while Alaric stood guard near the door, his eyes scanning the shadows.

Sylvara settled across from Elara, her blind gaze seeming to pierce her soul. "You carry the map of the ancients," she said, her voice a low chant. "It led you through the door, as the prophecy foretold."

Elara hesitated, then pulled the stone slab from her bag, its carvings faintly glowing in the library's light. "This? It's just something I found in a field."

Sylvara's fingers brushed the map, and a soft hum filled the air, the runes flaring briefly. "Not just anything," she murmured. "This is a relic of the First Mages, crafted to guide the dawnbringer to Aurora's heart. You are the one we've awaited."

Elara's throat tightened. "But why me? I'm no one special. I'm just a girl from a village."

Kael snorted. "A village girl who braved Brackenwood and walked through a magical door. Ordinary, my tail."

Sylvara's smile deepened. "The prophecy does not choose based on titles or power, but on heart. It speaks of a mortal who will wield the Heart of Radiance to break Morgath's curse and restore Liora's light."

Elara leaned forward, her curiosity overriding her doubt. "Tell me about the prophecy."

Sylvara's voice took on a rhythmic cadence, as if reciting from memory. "When twilight claims the land and shadows bind the heart, a dawnbringer shall cross the threshold, bearing the map of stars. Through trials of mind, spirit, and will, they shall seek the Heart of Radiance, a crystal born of Liora's soul. Only with courage and unity shall the curse be broken, and light reborn."

Elara's mind spun. Trials? Unity? The words felt heavy, like a mantle she wasn't ready to wear. "And if I fail?"

Sylvara's expression darkened. "Aurora will fall. Morgath will consume its magic, and her shadow may spread beyond this realm, to your world and beyond."

The thought of Briarwood—her parents, the fields, the clinic—tainted by Morgath's darkness made Elara's chest ache. She glanced at Alaric, whose face was unreadable, and Kael, whose usual grin had vanished.

"What are these trials?" she asked, her voice steady despite the fear coiling within her.

Sylvara gestured to a scroll on the table, its edges frayed. "The Heart lies beyond the Three Realms: the Labyrinth of Whispers, where doubts take form; the Vale of Shadows, where time bends and past sins resurface; and the Sky Spire, guarded by ancient protectors. Each will test you, dawnbringer."

Alaric spoke at last, his voice rough. "Morgath will know we seek the Heart. She'll send her forces to stop us."

Kael's ears twitched. "Which is why we need to move fast. Lumina's wards are weakening, and those wraiths weren't just passing by."

As if on cue, a low, guttural howl pierced the air outside, chilling Elara's blood. The floating orbs in the library flickered, and the wards outside pulsed erratically. Sylvara rose, her robes rustling. "They've come."

Alaric drew his sword, its blade catching the dim light. "Wraiths. More than before."

Elara's heart raced. "What do we do?"

Sylvara's voice was calm but urgent. "Flee. The library's wards will hold for now, but you must leave Lumina before Morgath's forces breach the village. Take the western path to the Starlit Vale—it's your first step toward the Three Realms."

Kael leapt from the table, his fur bristling. "Time to run, dawnbringer. Grab your map and let's go."

Elara stuffed the map into her bag, her hands shaking. As they hurried toward the library's rear exit, a crash echoed from the front, followed by a chorus of hisses. The wards flared, then dimmed, their light faltering under an unseen assault.

Alaric pushed open the back door, revealing a narrow alley lined with glowing vines. "Stay behind me," he ordered, leading the way.

They ran, the cobblestones slick under Elara's boots. The village was chaos—villagers shouting, wards crackling, and the howls of shadow-wraiths growing louder. Elara's lungs burned, but she kept pace, Kael darting at her side, his eyes scanning the shadows.

As they reached the village's edge, a wraith lunged from an alley, its form a writhing mass of darkness with glowing eyes. Alaric swung his sword, the blade slicing through the creature, which dissolved into smoke with a piercing shriek. But more hisses echoed from the trees beyond the wards.

"Keep moving!" Alaric shouted, shoving Elara forward.

They plunged into the forest, the wards' glow fading behind them. The path to the Starlit Vale was barely visible, overgrown with roots and thorns. Elara's heart pounded, not just from fear but from the weight of the prophecy now etched in her mind. She was the dawnbringer, chosen or not, and Aurora's fate rested on her shoulders.

As they vanished into the trees, a wraith perched on a branch above Lumina, its eyes fixed on their retreating forms. It let out a low, guttural whisper, carried on the wind to its mistress: "They seek the Heart."

Chapter 7:

The Quest Begins

The forest swallowed Elara, Kael, and Ser Alaric as they fled Lumina, the village's flickering wards fading into the twilight behind them. The air was thick with the scent of pine and damp earth, laced with the metallic tang of Aurora's fading magic. The path to the Starlit Vale was barely a trail, overgrown with thorns and roots that snagged at Elara's cloak. Her heart pounded, not just from the sprint but from the weight of Sylvara's words—the prophecy, the Heart of Radiance, the Three Realms. She was the dawnbringer, or so they claimed, but the title felt like a mantle too heavy for her shoulders.

Kael darted ahead, his orange fur a beacon in the dim light, his ears swiveling for signs of pursuit. "Keep moving, dawnbringer!" he called, his voice sharp but laced with his usual mischief. "Those wraiths don't take kindly to being outrun."

Elara's lungs burned, her boots slipping on the uneven ground. "I'm trying," she gasped, clutching the stone map in her bag. Its weight grounded her, a reminder of why she'd left Briarwood—chasing a legend that was now all too real.

Ser Alaric ran beside her, his scarred armor glinting faintly in the twilight. His sword was sheathed, but his hand rested on its hilt, ready for the next threat. "Stay alert," he said, his voice low and steady. "Morgath's minions won't stop at Lumina's borders."

The memory of the shadow-wraiths—those formless, ember-eyed creatures—sent a shiver down Elara's spine. She glanced back, half-expecting to see glowing eyes in the trees, but the forest was still, save for the rustle of leaves and the distant howl of a wraith, too far to pursue. For now.

They slowed as the path widened, the trees parting to reveal a clearing bathed in the glow of star-like flowers that pulsed softly in the grass. The Starlit Vale lay ahead, Sylvara had said, a stepping stone to the Three Realms. Elara caught her breath, her hands on her knees, and looked at her companions. Kael's tail flicked restlessly, while Alaric scanned the clearing, his face etched with a tension that hadn't eased since the library.

"Are we safe here?" Elara asked, her voice barely above a whisper.

Kael snorted, hopping onto a moss-covered rock. "Safe? In Aurora? That's like asking if a dragon's friendly. We're just less likely to be eaten here."

Alaric's eyes softened slightly, a rare flicker of warmth. "The Vale's magic is older, stronger. Morgath's influence is weaker here, but we can't linger. We need supplies and a plan before we face the Three Realms."

Elara nodded, her mind racing. The Labyrinth of Whispers, the Vale of Shadows, the Sky Spire—each trial sounded more daunting than the last. "What kind of supplies?" she asked. "And where do we get them?"

"There's a settlement nearby," Alaric said, pointing toward a faint glow beyond the clearing. "A trading post, neutral ground. We'll find food, weapons, maybe information."

Kael's ears twitched. "And maybe someone who doesn't scream 'outsider' the moment they see you, dawnbringer. No offense, but you stick out like a turnip in a rose garden."

Elara managed a small smile, despite the weight in her chest. "Thanks for the confidence boost."

Kael's grin was all teeth. "Anytime."

As they moved toward the settlement, Elara felt a pang of homesickness. She thought of her parents— her father's calloused hands guiding the plow, her mother's gentle touch at the clinic. Would they be worried, wondering where she'd gone? She pushed the thought aside. She was here now, in a world of glowing rivers and dying magic, and she had to keep moving.

The trading post was a cluster of tents and wooden stalls, lit by floating lanterns that bobbed like fireflies. Merchants in vibrant cloaks haggled over goods—crystals that hummed with energy, herbs that glowed faintly, blades etched with runes. The air buzzed with voices, some melodic, others sharp, and Elara caught snippets of languages she couldn't understand. The people were as varied as the wares—some with skin like polished stone, others with eyes that shimmered like the rivers. All of them glanced at her, their curiosity tinged with suspicion.

Alaric led them to a stall manned by a wiry man with a shock of silver hair and a sly smile. "Toren," Alaric greeted, his tone guarded. "We need provisions for a journey—food, water, a map of the Vale."

Toren's eyes flicked to Elara, lingering on her plain cloak and the bag slung over her shoulder. "And who's this? A mortal in Aurora? Bold choice, Alaric."

"She's with us," Alaric said, his voice firm. "Can you help or not?"

Toren chuckled, spreading his hands. "For you, old friend? Always. But it'll cost you."

Kael leapt onto the stall's counter, his tail brushing a stack of herbs. "Don't play games, Toren. We're on a tight schedule, and Morgath's wraiths aren't exactly patient."

Toren's smile faltered at the mention of Morgath. "Fine. Bread, dried fruit, a waterskin, and a map. I'll throw in some starbloom salve for wounds—on the house." He began gathering items, his movements swift but nervous.

Elara watched him closely, a prickle of unease at the back of her neck. Something about his quick glances and forced cheer felt off, but she couldn't place it. As Toren handed her a waterskin, his fingers brushed hers, and she caught a flicker of something in his eyes—guilt, perhaps, or fear.

"Thank you," she said, keeping her tone polite but guarded.

Toren nodded, avoiding her gaze. "Safe travels, mortal. You'll need it."

As they moved away from the stall, Elara leaned toward Kael. "Is he trustworthy?" she whispered.

Kael's ears flicked. "Toren's a survivor. He'll sell to anyone with coin, but he's no hero. Keep an eye on him."

They continued through the trading post, gathering a few more supplies—a dagger for Elara, its hilt carved with a crescent moon; a cloak for Alaric, woven with threads that shimmered faintly; and a small pouch of glowing seeds Kael insisted were "useful in a pinch." Elara's bag grew heavier, but so did her resolve. Each item felt like a step toward the Heart of Radiance, toward saving Aurora.

As they prepared to leave, Alaric pulled Elara aside, his voice low. "I owe you an explanation," he said, his eyes shadowed. "I was part of Liora's guard when Morgath betrayed her. I failed to protect her, and I was exiled for it. This quest... it's my chance to make things right."

Elara's heart ached at the pain in his voice. "You're here now," she said softly. "That's what matters."

He nodded, a flicker of gratitude in his eyes, but before he could respond, Kael hissed, "Trouble!"

Elara turned to see Toren speaking to a cloaked figure at the edge of the trading post, his gestures furtive. The figure's hood concealed their face, but a chill ran through Elara as she caught a glimpse of ember-like eyes beneath it. A shadow-wraith.

"He's betraying us," Kael growled, his fur bristling. "Toren's sold us out."

Alaric's hand flew to his sword. "We move. Now."

They sprinted toward the forest, the trading post's lanterns fading behind them. The air grew colder, the twilight darker, as if Morgath's influence was closing in. Elara's heart raced, her mind reeling. Toren had seemed kind, helpful—how could he turn on them so quickly?

As they plunged into the trees, the hissing of wraiths echoed behind them, closer than before. Alaric led the way, hacking through vines with his sword, while Kael darted beside Elara, his eyes scanning the shadows. "The Vale's just ahead," he panted. "If we reach it, we can lose them."

Elara's legs burned, but she pushed on, the prophecy's words echoing in her mind: "courage and unity". She glanced at Alaric, his face set with determination, and Kael, his usual jest replaced by fierce focus. They were her allies, her strength. She wouldn't let them down.

But as they broke through the trees into the Starlit Vale—a vast expanse of glowing flowers and shimmering mist—the hissing grew louder, and a dozen ember-eyes gleamed in the darkness behind them. Toren's betrayal had brought Morgath's forces closer than ever, and the path to the Three Realms was no longer a distant challenge—it was a race for survival.

Chapter 8:

The Labyrinth of Whispers

The Starlit Vale shimmered behind Elara, Kael, and Ser Alaric as they plunged deeper into the forest, the hissing of shadow-wraiths fading but not forgotten. The betrayal at the trading post—Toren's sly glance to the cloaked wraith—still stung, a reminder of Morgath's reach. Elara's breath came in sharp gasps, her legs aching from the sprint, but she pushed forward, the stone map heavy in her bag. The prophecy's weight pressed harder: "Through trials of mind, spirit, and will, the dawnbringer shall seek the Heart of Radiance". The first trial, the Labyrinth of Whispers, loomed ahead, its entrance hidden in the Vale's misty heart.

Kael darted through the underbrush, his orange fur a flickering beacon in the twilight. "Almost there," he called, his voice taut but laced with his usual spark. "The Labyrinth's entrance is finicky—blinks in and out like a bad dream. Stay sharp."

Elara nodded, brushing sweat from her brow. The air grew thicker, heavy with a mist that swirled like liquid silver, muffling the hum of Aurora's magic. The trees here were ancient, their trunks twisted into shapes that seemed to watch her, their glowing leaves dimming as if wary of what lay ahead.

Ser Alaric strode beside her, his scarred armor glinting faintly. His silence was heavier since the trading post, his gray eyes scanning the shadows. Elara wanted to ask about his exile, about the guilt he'd hinted at, but the urgency of their flight left no room for words. Instead, she drew strength from his steady presence, a rock against the tide of her doubts.

The path ended abruptly at a clearing where the mist parted, revealing a stone archway carved with runes that pulsed like heartbeats. Beyond it, a maze of towering hedges stretched into the distance, their leaves shimmering with an eerie, greenish glow. The air within buzzed with faint whispers—fragments of voices, too soft to discern but sharp enough to prickle Elara's skin.

"The Labyrinth of Whispers," Alaric said, his voice low. "The first trial. It tests the mind, conjuring doubts and fears. Whatever you hear, whatever you see, don't trust it."

Kael's ears twitched, his grin strained. "Sounds like a party. Just don't go running off if you hear your mum calling you for supper."

Elara managed a weak smile, but her stomach churned. She wasn't a hero, not really—just a girl from Briarwood who'd stumbled into a prophecy. What if the Labyrinth saw through her, exposed her as unworthy? She gripped the map tighter, its cool stone grounding her. "How do we find the way through?" she asked.

Alaric's eyes met hers, steady but grave. "The Labyrinth shifts, but the Heart's path is tied to truth. Trust your heart, dawnbringer. It's stronger than you know."

Kael hopped onto a nearby root. "And stick together. The whispers love to split groups—makes it easier to mess with your head."

With a deep breath, Elara stepped toward the archway, her companions flanking her. As they crossed the threshold, the runes flared, and a cold wind swept through, carrying a chorus of whispers that coiled around her like smoke. ""You're not enough,"" they hissed. ""A farmer's daughter, playing at hero. You'll fail them all.""

Elara flinched, her step faltering. The voices sounded so real, like her own thoughts given form. She glanced at Kael and Alaric, but their faces were set, their own battles hidden behind tight jaws and narrowed eyes.

The hedges loomed, their leaves rustling as if alive, the path branching into a dozen twisting corridors. The whispers grew louder, weaving doubts into a suffocating tapestry. ""Why did you leave Briarwood? Your parents need you. You're selfish, chasing dreams."" Elara's chest tightened, memories of her mother's clinic, her father's fields, flashing in her mind.

"Shut up," she muttered, shaking her head. Kael glanced at her, his eyes sharp.

"Hearing them already?" he asked, his tone lighter than his expression. "They're just noise, dawnbringer. Keep moving."

But the whispers didn't stop. As they navigated the maze, the paths shifted, walls sliding silently to block their way or open new routes. Elara's heart raced, her sense of direction unraveling. Then, a new voice cut through—a voice she knew too well.

"Elara, why did you abandon us?" It was her mother, Mara, her tone soft but laced with pain.

Elara froze, her breath hitching. Ahead, the mist parted, revealing a figure in the shadows—Mara, her silver-streaked braid glinting, her brown eyes filled with disappointment. "You left us to chase a fairy tale," the vision said. "We're struggling without you."

"It's not real," Alaric growled, grabbing her arm. "Keep walking."

But Elara couldn't tear her eyes away. The vision felt so vivid, the guilt so sharp. "I didn't mean to," she whispered, her voice breaking. "I just wanted—"

"Wanted what?" another voice snapped—her father, Thom, stepping from the mist beside Mara. "To be more than us? You're no hero, Elara. You're a dreamer who'll get herself killed."

Tears stung Elara's eyes. She knew it was the Labyrinth, knew these were lies, but the words dug deep, unearthing fears she'd buried. What if she was abandoning her family? What if she wasn't enough?

Kael's tail brushed her leg, grounding her. "They're not your parents," he said, his voice firm but kind. "You're here to save Aurora, to save "them". Don't let the whispers win."

Elara nodded, wiping her eyes. She forced herself to turn away, the visions fading into mist. But the whispers shifted, targeting her companions. A new voice—cold, feminine—hissed at Alaric. ""You failed Liora. You let Morgath take her. You're a coward.""

Alaric's step faltered, his face paling. Elara saw the pain in his eyes, the same guilt he'd confessed at the trading post. "Alaric," she said, reaching for his arm. "It's not true. You're fighting for her now."

He met her gaze, his expression raw, then nodded curtly, pressing on. The whispers turned to Kael next, their tone mocking. ""Trickster, liar, useless fox. You'll betray them, just like always.""

Kael's grin vanished, his ears flattening. "Not today," he muttered, but Elara caught the flicker of doubt in his eyes.

The maze tightened around them, the hedges closing in, the whispers a relentless storm. Elara's head throbbed, her doubts threatening to overwhelm her. Then, a new vision appeared—a mirror-like surface in the hedge, reflecting not her face but a version of herself: weak, trembling, alone. ""You'll fail,'" the reflection sneered. "'You're not the dawnbringer. You're nothing.'"

Elara's knees buckled, but she caught herself, anger flaring. "No," she said, her voice rising. "I'm here. I crossed the door. I faced the wraiths. I'm "trying"." She stepped toward the reflection, her fists clenched. "I'm enough."

The mirror shattered, the shards dissolving into mist. The whispers faltered, the hedges parting to reveal a stone pedestal at the Labyrinth's heart. On it rested a single, glowing rune—a symbol of passage, pulsing with soft light.

Kael let out a low whistle. "Well, look at that. You told the Labyrinth who's boss."

Elara's chest heaved, her body trembling but her resolve stronger. "Is that it? Did we pass?"

Alaric nodded, his voice gruff but proud. "The Labyrinth tests truth. You faced your doubts and stood firm. The first trial is yours."

They approached the pedestal, the rune's light bathing them in warmth. As Elara touched it, a pulse of energy surged through her, and the hedges parted, revealing a path leading out of the maze. Beyond, the

Starlit Vale shimmered, the next trial—the Vale of Shadows—waiting.

But as they stepped forward, a low hiss echoed from the shadows behind them. Elara spun, her heart leaping. A shadow-wraith slithered from the mist, its ember-eyes locked on her. "The dawnbringer," it rasped, its voice like breaking glass. "Morgath sees you."

Alaric drew his sword, Kael's fur bristling. The wraith lunged, and the Labyrinth's whispers rose again, a final taunt as the battle began.

Chapter 9:

The Vale of Shadows

Elara's heart thundered as she ducked under Ser Alaric's sweeping sword, the blade slicing through the shadow-wraith that had lunged from the Labyrinth's mist. The creature dissolved into a hiss of black smoke, its ember-eyes fading, but the echoes of its rasping voice—"Morgath sees you"—lingered in her mind. The Labyrinth of Whispers was behind them, its glowing hedges and taunting voices vanquished, but the victory felt fleeting as they stumbled onto the path leading to the Vale of Shadows.

The air grew colder, the twilight of Aurora deepening into a murky gloom as the trio pressed forward. The Starlit Vale's glowing flowers and shimmering mist gave way to a landscape of gnarled, leafless trees, their branches clawing at a sky bruised with swirling grays. The ground was soft, almost spongy, and a faint, metallic scent hung in the air, mingling with the distant wail of a wind that never touched them. Elara clutched the stone map, its carvings now a dull pulse, as if wary of the realm they approached.

Kael padded beside her, his orange fur dimmed in the oppressive light, his usual grin replaced by a tense frown. "Welcome to the Vale of Shadows," he muttered, his ears twitching. "Where time plays tricks and the past comes back to bite you. Literally, sometimes."

Elara's stomach knotted. The Labyrinth had tested her mind, conjuring doubts that nearly broke her. What would this place do? She glanced at Ser Alaric, his scarred face set in a grim mask, his hand still gripping his sword. The wraith's attack had shaken him, though he hid it well. "What kind of trial is this?" she asked, her voice steadier than she felt.

Alaric's gray eyes flicked to her, shadowed with something deeper than caution. "The Vale bends time," he said, his voice rough. "It drags up the past—mistakes, regrets, things you'd rather forget. To pass, you must face them and move forward."

Kael snorted, though it lacked his usual spark. "Sounds delightful. Just don't expect me to spill my secrets, dawnbringer. I've got too many to sort through."

Elara managed a small smile, but her nerves tightened. Her past wasn't filled with grand tragedies—she was just a girl from Briarwood—but the guilt of leaving her parents, the fear of not being enough, gnawed at her. What would the Vale show her? And what haunted her companions?

The path descended into a ravine, where the air grew heavy, pressing against Elara's chest like a physical weight. The ground shimmered, rippling like a pond disturbed by a stone, and the trees seemed to shift, their branches forming fleeting shapes— faces, hands, moments frozen in time. The whispers from the Labyrinth were gone, replaced by a silence so profound it felt alive.

As they reached the ravine's heart, the ground pulsed, and a wave of dizziness washed over Elara. She stumbled, her vision blurring, and when it cleared, she was no longer in the ravine. She stood in Briarwood, in her mother's clinic, the familiar scent of herbs and antiseptic filling her lungs. Her mother, Mara, knelt beside a patient—a young boy with a fevered brow—her hands trembling with exhaustion.

"Elara," Mara said, her voice sharp with reproach. "Where were you? I needed you here, and you ran off chasing dreams."

Elara's throat tightened. "Mama, I—"

"You left us," her father's voice cut in, Thom appearing beside Mara, his hazel eyes heavy with disappointment. "The fields are failing without you. You abandoned your duty."

The words struck like a blade, echoing the doubts the Labyrinth had conjured. Elara reached out, desperate to explain, but her parents faded, the clinic dissolving into mist. She was back in the Vale, her companions staring at her with concern.

"You saw something," Alaric said, not a question. His face was pale, his grip on his sword tightening.

Elara nodded, her voice shaky. "My parents. They said I abandoned them."

Kael's tail flicked, his eyes softening. "The Vale's a liar, dawnbringer. It twists the past to hurt you. Keep walking."

But before they could move, the ground rippled again, and Alaric froze, his eyes widening. The air shimmered, and a vision coalesced—a woman with flowing silver hair and eyes like starlight, standing in a radiant hall. Princess Liora. Beside her stood a younger Alaric, his armor gleaming, his face unscarred and full of devotion.

"You failed me," Liora's voice echoed, cold and accusing. "You swore to protect me, and you let Morgath take my soul."

Alaric's knees buckled, his sword clattering to the ground. "Liora," he whispered, his voice raw. "I tried. I—"

"You loved her," Liora's vision continued, her form shifting to reveal another figure—Morgath, her dark beauty stark against Liora's light. "You loved Morgath, and you couldn't stop her. You're weak, Alaric."

Elara's heart ached at the pain in Alaric's eyes. She stepped toward him, her hand brushing his arm. "It's not real," she said, echoing his words from the Labyrinth. "You're here now, fighting for her."

Alaric's breath hitched, and he tore his gaze from the vision, which dissolved into mist. "She's right," he said, his voice hoarse. "Morgath was... my love, once. Before she turned to darkness. I couldn't see it then, but I see it now."

The admission hung heavy, and Elara squeezed his arm, her empathy overriding her fear. "You're not that man anymore," she said softly. "You're fighting to make it right."

Kael, silent until now, flinched as the ground rippled beneath him. A vision formed—a younger Kael, smaller and less vibrant, cowering before a towering figure cloaked in shadow. "You're nothing but a trickster," the figure sneered. "You'll betray them all, just like you betrayed me."

Kael's fur bristled, his eyes flashing with defiance. "Not this time," he growled, and the vision shattered, leaving him trembling but resolute.

Elara's chest tightened. The Vale was relentless, exposing their deepest wounds. But as they stood together, their shared vulnerability forged a bond stronger than the trial's cruelty. "We can do this," she said, her voice firm. "Together."

The ground pulsed once more, and Elara's vision shifted again. This time, she saw herself—younger, sitting by her father's side as he told stories of Aurora. "You're destined for more," he said, his voice warm. The memory was real, not a taunt, and it steadied her. She hadn't abandoned her parents— she was honoring their belief in her.

The Vale seemed to sense her resolve. The ground stabilized, and a path appeared, leading to a stone archway etched with runes, its center glowing with a soft, silver light. "The exit," Alaric said, retrieving his sword. "You've faced the past, dawnbringer. You've passed the second trial."

Elara nodded, her heart lighter but her body weary. They stepped toward the archway, the Vale's oppressive air lifting slightly. But as they neared, a low, guttural hiss slithered from the shadows. A shadow-wraith emerged, larger than the others, its form more solid, its ember-eyes blazing with malice.

"Dawnbringer," it rasped, its voice a jagged blade. "Morgath's patience wanes."

Alaric raised his sword, Kael's claws unsheathed, and Elara gripped her dagger, her pulse racing. The wraith lunged, and the Vale erupted into chaos, the trial's end marked not by peace but by battle.

Chapter 10:

The Skyward Path

The Starlit Vale shimmered below as Elara trudged up a winding path, her boots crunching on crystalline gravel that sparkled like fallen stars. The Vale of Shadows' oppressive gloom had lifted, its visions of guilt and regret fading like a bad dream, but the shadow-wraith's final hiss—"Morgath's patience wanes"—clung to her thoughts like damp mist. The stone map pulsed faintly in her hands, its runes guiding them toward the Sky Spire, the final trial where the Heart of Radiance awaited. Her heart raced with equal parts hope and dread. Two trials conquered, one to go—but at what cost?

Kael scampered ahead, his orange fur catching the twilight's glow, his tail flicking with restless energy. "Pick up the pace, dawnbringer!" he called, his voice lighter than his wary eyes suggested. "The Spire's not going to climb itself, and I'd rather not meet more of Morgath's pets."

Elara managed a weak smile, her legs aching from the Vale's ordeal. "I'm moving, trickster," she said, gripping her dagger's hilt for comfort. The weapon, traded for at Lumina's outpost, felt heavier now, as if it knew the battles ahead.

Ser Alaric walked beside her, his scarred armor clinking softly, his gray eyes scanning the horizon. The Vale had exposed his past—his love for Morgath, his failure to save Liora—and though he stood tall, a quiet weight lingered in his silence. Elara wanted to ease his burden, but the path demanded their focus. She glanced at him, catching a flicker of resolve in his gaze, and felt a surge of gratitude for his steadfast presence.

The path steepened, weaving through jagged outcrops that jutted like the bones of some ancient beast. The air grew thinner, tinged with a metallic tang, and the Vale's glowing flora gave way to bare stone, etched with faded runes that whispered of forgotten heroes. The map's glow intensified, pointing to a cliff's edge where the ground fell away into a swirling abyss of clouds. Above, the Sky Spire loomed—a floating citadel of glass-like stone, its towers piercing the twilight sky, connected by bridges that shimmered like gossamer threads.

Elara's breath caught. "It's... impossible," she whispered, her voice swallowed by the wind.

Kael snorted, leaping onto a nearby rock. "Impossible's just another word for 'fun,' dawnbringer. Besides, that's where the Heart is, so unless you fancy letting Morgath win…"

Alaric's hand rested on his sword. "Veyra guards the Heart," he said, his voice low. "A dragon of fire and wisdom. She'll test your worth, Elara, not just your strength."

Elara's stomach knotted. A dragon? The Labyrinth had twisted her mind, the Vale her heart—what would this trial demand? She thought of Briarwood, her parents' faces, and the prophecy Sylvara had unveiled: *"Only through courage and unity shall the curse be broken."* She wasn't alone. That had to count for something.

The map pulsed, revealing a hidden staircase carved into the cliff, its steps glowing faintly. "Let's go," Elara said, her voice steadier than she felt. She led the way, each step a defiance of her fear.

The staircase spiraled upward, its edges crumbling into the abyss below. Wind howled, tugging at Elara's cloak, and the Spire's towers seemed to shift, their reflections dancing in the clouds. Kael's claws scrabbled on the stone, his usual banter subdued, while Alaric's armor clinked rhythmically, a grounding presence. Halfway up, the staircase trembled, and a low rumble echoed from above.

"Wraiths?" Elara asked, her dagger drawn, eyes scanning the mist.

Alaric's gaze narrowed. "No. Something older."

The rumble grew, and a massive shape uncoiled from a tower's base—a creature of molten gold scales, its wings folded, its eyes twin flames that burned through the twilight. Veyra. The dragon's presence was a physical weight, pressing against Elara's chest, but her voice, when it spoke, was a deep, resonant melody that vibrated in her bones.

"Dawnbringer," Veyra rumbled, her gaze locking onto Elara. "You seek the Heart of Radiance. Why?"

Elara's throat tightened, but she stepped forward, the map's glow steadying her. "To save Aurora," she said, her voice clear. "To free Princess Liora from Morgath's curse."

Veyra's tail flicked, sparks flying. "Many have sought the Heart. All failed. What makes you worthy?"

Kael's ears twitched, his grin nervous. "She's got a knack for not dying, if that helps."

Alaric shot him a look, then faced Veyra. "She's faced trials you'd respect, dragon. Her heart is true."

Elara's chest warmed at their words, but Veyra's eyes bore into her, unyielding. "Words are wind," the dragon said. "Show me."

The ground pulsed, and the staircase vanished, leaving Elara, Kael, and Alaric on a floating platform of glass-like stone, the abyss yawning below. The air shimmered, and visions appeared—Briarwood's fields burning, her parents trapped in flames; Alaric facing Morgath, his sword breaking; Kael cowering before a shadowed figure, his defiance crumbling. Elara's heart raced, recognizing the Vale's trickery, but these visions felt sharper, more real.

"This is your trial," Veyra said. "Face your fears, not as shadows, but as truths. Fail, and the Spire claims you."

Elara's vision blurred, and she stood in Briarwood, flames licking the sky. Her mother's voice echoed: "You left us to die." She clutched the map, its warmth grounding her. "It's not real," she whispered, stepping through the flames, which parted like mist. She emerged on the platform, trembling but whole.

Alaric faced his vision—Morgath's cruel smile, her voice taunting: "You'll always fail her." He roared, his sword slashing through the illusion, his face etched with pain but resolve. Kael's vision was quieter—a shadowed figure sneering, "You're nothing." He bared his teeth, leaping through the shadow, landing with a defiant snarl.

Veyra's eyes softened, a flicker of approval. "You face truths and stand. But one test remains."

The platform shuddered, and a bridge of light appeared, leading to the Spire's heart. At its end, a pedestal glowed, the Heart of Radiance pulsing within—a crystal of starlight, its facets reflecting Liora's trapped soul. But as Elara stepped forward, a shadow-wraith materialized, larger than any before, its ember-eyes blazing with Morgath's malice.

"Dawnbringer," it hissed. "The Heart is ours."

Alaric raised his sword, Kael's claws unsheathed, and Elara gripped her dagger, her pulse thundering. The wraith lunged, and the Spire erupted into battle, the Heart's light flickering as darkness closed in.

Chapter 11:

The Heart's Betrayal

The wind howled around Elara as she clung to the narrow stone ledge of the Sky Spire, her fingers numb from the biting cold. The floating citadel loomed above, its jagged towers piercing the twilight sky of Aurora like shards of glass. Below, clouds swirled in an endless abyss, hiding the Starlit Vale and the trials they'd conquered—the Labyrinth of Whispers and the Vale of Shadows. Her heart pounded, not just from the dizzying height but from the weight of their mission: the Heart of Radiance, the crystal that could break Morgath's curse and free Princess Liora, was within reach.

Kael scrambled ahead, his orange fur ruffled by the gusts, his claws gripping the rock with uncanny grace. "Almost there, dawnbringer!" he called, his voice nearly lost in the wind. "Unless you'd rather take a scenic dive into the void."

Elara forced a shaky smile, her breath misting in the frigid air. "Not today," she muttered, pulling herself higher. The dagger at her hip—gifted at the trading post—bumped against her thigh, a small comfort against the trials behind and the unknown ahead.

Ser Alaric climbed beside her, his scarred armor scraping the stone. His gray eyes were fixed on the spire's peak, but the tension in his jaw betrayed his unease. The Vale of Shadows had shaken him, unearthing his past love for Morgath and his failure to save Liora. Elara wanted to reassure him, but the climb demanded all her focus.

The ledge widened into a platform carved with runes that pulsed faintly, like dying embers. Above, a spiral staircase wound into the spire's heart, its steps floating without visible support. Elara's stomach lurched at the sight, but Kael was already bounding upward, his tail a flicker of fire in the gloom.

"Veyra's lair is at the top," Alaric said, his voice low. "The dragon guards the Heart. She'll test you, dawnbringer. Be ready."

Elara nodded, her throat tight. A dragon. After facing whispers and shadows, a creature of fire and scale felt impossibly daunting. But she'd come too far to falter. She stepped onto the first stair, its surface solid despite its ethereal glow, and began the ascent.

The staircase spiraled through a vast chamber, its walls shimmering with constellations that seemed to shift, telling stories of Aurora's past. The air grew warmer, tinged with the scent of ash and molten stone. At the peak, the chamber opened into a circular arena, its floor inlaid with a mosaic of a radiant heart. In the center, coiled on a pedestal of obsidian, was Veyra—a dragon with scales like molten gold, her eyes twin flames that burned into Elara's soul.

"Welcome, dawnbringer," Veyra's voice rumbled, deep and resonant, shaking the air. "You seek the Heart of Radiance."

Elara's knees trembled, but she stood tall, her companions flanking her. "We need it to save Aurora," she said, her voice steadier than she felt. "To free Princess Liora from Morgath's curse."

Veyra's tail flicked, sparks flying where it struck the stone. "Many have sought the Heart. Few have been worthy. Prove your selflessness, mortal, or perish."

Kael's ears twitched, his grin nervous. "No pressure, right?"

Veyra's gaze shifted to him, then back to Elara. "A memory," she said. "Give me your most cherished moment, willingly surrendered, to show you value others above yourself."

Elara's heart sank. A memory? She thought of her parents—her father's stories by the fire, her mother's gentle hands teaching her to bandage wounds. One moment stood out: a summer evening when she was ten, her parents laughing as they danced in the fields under a starlit sky, pulling her into their embrace. It was her anchor, her reminder of home.

But Aurora was dying. Liora was trapped. She closed her eyes, the memory's warmth flooding her, then let it go, offering it to Veyra like a fragile gift. Pain lanced through her, a hollow ache where the memory had been, but she stood firm.

Veyra's eyes softened, a flicker of respect. "You are worthy," she rumbled. The pedestal glowed, and a crystal rose from its center—the Heart of Radiance, pulsing with light like a captured star, its facets reflecting fragments of Liora's soul.

Elara reached for it, her fingers trembling. The crystal was warm, its light flooding her with hope. "We did it," she whispered, turning to Kael and Alaric.

Kael's grin was triumphant. "Told you, dawnbringer. You're—"

A blast of dark energy shattered the moment, hurling Elara to the ground. The Heart slipped from her grasp, skidding across the mosaic. A figure materialized in the chamber's entrance—Morgath, her black robes swirling like smoke, her eyes glowing with malevolent power. Her beauty was stark, her silver hair a cruel echo of Liora's, but her presence was a void, draining the air of warmth.

"Foolish child," Morgath hissed, her voice a blade of ice. "You thought you could take what's mine?"

Alaric drew his sword, stepping in front of Elara. "You'll not have the Heart," he growled, though his voice trembled with old wounds.

Kael snarled, his claws unsheathed, but Morgath's gaze pinned him like a moth. "Stay, trickster," she sneered, and an invisible force slammed him against the wall.

Elara scrambled to her feet, her dagger in hand, but Morgath's power was overwhelming. The sorceress glided forward, her hand closing around the Heart. "You've done well to bring it to me," she said, her smile cruel. "Join me, dawnbringer. Rule Aurora at my side, and I'll spare your pathetic companions."

Elara's blood ran cold. Rule Aurora? The idea was absurd, but Morgath's voice wormed into her mind, promising power, safety, an end to the fear. She thought of Briarwood, her parents—could she protect them by giving in? But then she saw Alaric's defiant stance, Kael struggling against the spell, and the Heart's light dimming in Morgath's grip.

"No," Elara said, her voice ringing with resolve. "I'll never join you."

Morgath's smile vanished. "Then watch them die." She raised her hand, dark energy crackling, but before she could strike, Elara lunged, her dagger slashing at Morgath's arm. The blade barely grazed her, but it was enough to break her focus.

The Heart fell, and Morgath snarled, seizing it again. With a flick of her wrist, she shattered the crystal, its shards scattering across the arena like falling stars. "You'll never have it," she spat, her form dissolving into smoke as she vanished, leaving only her laughter echoing in the chamber.

Elara dropped to her knees, her hands scrabbling for the shards, but they were cold, their light extinguished. "No," she whispered, tears stinging her eyes. The Heart was gone, their hope shattered.

Kael staggered free, his fur matted, his eyes wide. "She... she broke it."

Alaric's face was ashen, his sword lowered. "We failed," he murmured, the words heavy with despair.

But as Elara clutched a shard, a faint warmth pulsed against her palm. She looked up, her voice trembling but fierce. "We're not done. We'll find another way."

Before they could respond, a shadow-wraith slithered into the chamber, its ember-eyes gleaming. Morgath's voice echoed through it: "Run, dawnbringer. My patience is at an end."

The wraith lunged, and Elara was yanked back by Alaric as they fled down the staircase, the spire trembling around them. The Heart was lost, Morgath's power unchecked, but Elara's resolve burned brighter than ever. The fight was far from over.

Chapter 12:

Shattered but Not Broken

The Sky Spire trembled as Elara stumbled down the floating staircase, her heart pounding in her ears. The air was thick with the acrid scent of Morgath's dark magic, the echo of her cruel laughter lingering like a venomous fog. Behind her, Ser Alaric's armored steps thundered, his sword drawn against the shadow-wraith that pursued them. Kael darted at her side, his orange fur matted, his usual mischief replaced by a fierce determination. The Heart of Radiance—shattered into lifeless shards by Morgath's hand—was gone, their hope seemingly crushed. Yet Elara clutched a single fragment in her fist, its faint warmth a flicker of defiance against the despair threatening to swallow her.

"Move, dawnbringer!" Kael hissed, his claws scrabbling on the glowing steps. "That wraith's not here for a chat!"

Elara's legs burned, her breath ragged as they descended into the spire's lower chamber, its constellation-laden walls now dimmed, as if mourning the Heart's loss. The wraith's guttural hiss grew closer, its ember-eyes glinting in the shadows above. Alaric spun, his blade slashing through the air, but the creature dissolved into smoke, re-forming just out of reach.

"We can't fight it here," Alaric growled, shoving Elara toward a narrow archway at the chamber's edge. "To the Vale!"

They burst into the open air, the Starlit Vale sprawling below, its glowing flowers a fragile beacon in Aurora's endless twilight. The wind tore at Elara's cloak as they scrambled down a rocky path carved into the spire's base. But before they could reach the safety of the mist, a pulse of dark energy erupted behind them. Morgath's voice slithered through the air, cold and commanding: "Seize the dawnbringer."

Shadow-wraiths materialized, their forms more solid than before, their claws glinting like obsidian. Elara's dagger was useless against their speed. She ducked a slashing claw, but another wraith's tendril wrapped around her wrist, yanking her off her feet. Pain seared through her arm as she hit the ground, the shard slipping from her grasp.

"Elara!" Alaric roared, his sword cleaving through a wraith, but more surged forward, overwhelming him. Kael leapt, his teeth sinking into a wraith's smoky form, but a blast of energy sent him sprawling.

Elara struggled, her vision swimming, but the wraiths were relentless. A cold, invisible force tightened around her, and the world went black.

When Elara woke, her head throbbed, and her wrists ached from tight, glowing cords that bound her to a stone chair. She was in a cavern, its walls slick with moisture and etched with runes that pulsed a sickly red. Torches cast jagged shadows, and the air was heavy with the stench of damp earth and something darker—Morgath's corruption. Her bag was gone, the map with it, but the shard of the Heart was nowhere to be seen. Panic clawed at her chest. Where were Alaric and Kael?

A soft scrape drew her attention. Kael crouched in a cage of twisted vines across the cavern, his fur dull, his eyes sharp with worry. "Morning, dawnbringer," he whispered, his voice strained but warm. "Fancy meeting you here."

"Kael!" Elara rasped, her throat dry. "Where's Alaric? What is this place?"

Kael's ears flicked, his gaze dartingering. to the shadows. "No sign of Alaric—probably fighting his way out or captured somewhere else. As for this charming spot, I'd guess it's one of Morgath's lairs, deep under the Vale. She's got a thing for dramatic prisons."

Elara tugged at her bonds, but the glowing ropes tightened, stinging her skin. "She broke the Heart. We failed."

Kael's grin was faint but defiant. "Failed? You're still breathing, aren't you? And that shard you were clutching—did you hide it?"

Elara's heart skipped. She'd slipped the shard into a hidden seam in her cloak during the attack, a desperate act before she'd blacked out. She felt its faint warmth against her side, undetected by the wraiths. "It's still here," she whispered, hope flickering. "But what good is it do? The Heart's power is gone."

Kael's eyes gleamed with cunning. "Is it? The prophecy said the Heart's about light, about unity. Not just a shiny rock. You're the dawnbringer, Elara. The power's in you—us, this lot."

Elara's mind raced. Unity. Sylvara's words in the library echoed: ""Only through courage and unity shall the curse be broken."" The Heart wasn't just a crystal—it was a symbol, a catalyst to awaken Aurora's magic. Morgath had shattered the physical form, but could she break the spirit of the land's people? The villagers in Lumina, the traders, even Alaric and Kael—they all carried fragments of Aurora's light. If she could rally them…

"We have to get out of here," she said, her voice firming. "We need to find Alaric and the others."

Kael's tail flicked. "That's the spirit. Lucky for you, I'm a master at breaking out of cages." He twisted, his small paws working at the cage's vines, his claws picking at a weak knot. "Keep those wraiths distracted if they show up."

Elara scanned the cavern, her senses sharp. The runes pulsed erratically, and a distant hum suggested more wraiths nearby. She tested her bonds again, wincing as they burned, but noticed a faint crack in the chair's armrest. If she could leverage it…

A hiss interrupted her thoughts. A shadow-wraith slithered into the cavern, its ember-eyes locking onto her. "The dawnbringer wakes," it rasped, gliding closer. "Morgath will break you."

Elara's heart raced, but she forced her voice steady. "Tell Morgath she's wasting her time. I'm not giving up."

The wraith paused, its form flickering, as if surprised by her defiance. Behind it, Kael worked faster, a vine snapping free with a soft twang. Elara kept talking, buying time. "You're just her pawn, aren't you? Does she even care what happens to you?"

The wraith snarled, its claws extending, but Kael's cage burst open. He leapt, a blur of orange, his claws raking the wraith's back. It shrieked, dissolving into smoke, and Kael landed beside Elara, his breath ragged. "Nice distraction," he panted, slicing her bonds with a claw.

Elara rubbed her wrists, pain flaring but adrenaline surging. "Thanks," she said, retrieving the shard from her cloak. Its warmth steadied her. "Let's find Alaric and get out."

They crept through the cavern, Kael's nose twitching as he sniffed for danger. The tunnels twisted, their walls pulsing with Morgath's runes, but a faint breeze hinted at an exit. As they rounded a corner, they found Alaric—bound in a similar chair, his face bruised, his armor dented. His eyes widened at the sight of them.

"Elara," he rasped. "Kael. You're alive."

"Barely," Kael muttered, slicing Alaric's bonds. "No time for reunions. Morgath's got this place crawling with wraiths."

Alaric staggered to his feet, retrieving his sword from a nearby pile. "The Heart's gone," he said, his voice heavy. "What now?"

Elara held up the shard, its faint glow catching their eyes. "The Heart's power isn't in the crystal—it's in us, in Aurora's people. We rally them, channel their magic. We can still stop Morgath."

Alaric's gaze hardened, a flicker of hope returning. "Then we head to the Dawnfields. It's a gathering place for Aurora's outcasts. If we can unite them…"

Kael's grin returned, sharp and fierce. "A rebellion? Now you're speaking my language."

They moved toward the exit, the tunnels shaking as Morgath's magic stirred. A wraith's hiss echoed behind them, but they broke into a run, bursting into the Starlit Vale's misty air. The spire loomed above, a silent witness to their loss, but Elara's resolve burned bright. The Heart was shattered, but she was not. The fight for Aurora had just begun.

As they vanished into the mist, a wraith watched from the cavern's mouth, its whisper slithering to its mistress: "They rise."

Chapter 13:

Rallying the Realm

The Starlit Vale's mist swirled around Elara as she ran, her boots sinking into the glowing grass, the shard of the Heart of Radiance warm against her side. The cavern's damp chill clung to her skin, a reminder of their narrow escape from Morgath's lair. Behind her, Ser Alaric's armored steps were steady, his sword sheathed but his hand poised to draw it. Kael darted ahead, his orange fur a flicker in the twilight, his ears swiveling for signs of pursuit. The shadow-wraiths' hisses had faded, but Elara's heart still raced, Morgath's mocking voice—""Run, dawnbringer""—echoing in her mind.

The Heart was shattered, its power scattered, but Elara's resolve burned brighter than ever. Sylvara's prophecy had hinted at unity, and the shard's faint pulse told her the true strength lay not in the crystal but in Aurora's people. If they could rally the realm's outcasts, farmers, and healers, they might yet break Morgath's curse and free Princess Liora.

"Where exactly are these Dawnfields?" Elara panted, dodging a gnarled root. The Vale's glowing flowers dimmed in patches, Aurora's magic faltering under Morgath's grip.

Alaric's voice was gruff but steady. "A hidden plain beyond the Vale, where Aurora's rebels gather. It's a sanctuary, protected by old magic. Morgath's wraiths haven't found it—yet."

Kael leapt onto a fallen log, his grin sharp despite the tension. "It's also a mess of misfits who don't play well together. Farmers arguing with healers, outcasts bickering over scraps. Good luck getting them to agree on anything, dawnbringer."

Elara's stomach tightened. She was no leader—just a girl from Briarwood who'd stumbled into a prophecy. But she thought of her mother's calm authority in the clinic, her father's quiet strength in the fields. If she could channel that, maybe she could inspire Aurora's people. "We have to try," she said, her voice firm. "If we don't unite them, Morgath wins."

Alaric's gray eyes flicked to her, a flicker of pride breaking through his stoicism. "You're right. The Dawnfields are our last chance."

The path climbed, the mist thinning as the Vale gave way to a rocky ridge. Beyond, a plain stretched under Aurora's twilight sky, its grass shimmering with faint, golden light. Tents and makeshift shelters dotted the landscape, their glow fragile against the encroaching shadows. Figures moved among them—men and women with weary faces, children clutching glowing stones, all bearing the weight of a dying realm.

The Dawnfields. Elara's heart lifted, then sank. These were Aurora's last hope? They looked more like refugees than warriors.

As they descended, a tall woman with braided hair and a staff approached, her eyes sharp but wary. "Alaric," she greeted, her voice low. "Kael. And... a mortal?"

"This is Elara," Alaric said, stepping forward. "The dawnbringer."

Whispers rippled through the nearby crowd, some curious, others skeptical. The woman—introduced as Rhea, a healer from Lumina—studied Elara. "The prophecy speaks of you," she said, her tone guarded. "But words won't stop Morgath. What do you bring?"

Elara hesitated, then pulled the shard from her cloak, its faint glow catching the twilight. "The Heart of Radiance was shattered," she said, her voice steady despite the crowd's murmurs. "But its power lives in us—in you, in everyone here. Together, we can break Morgath's curse."

Rhea's eyes narrowed, but a flicker of hope crossed her face. "Bold words. Let's see if you can back them up."

They followed Rhea to a central tent, its interior lit by floating orbs. A dozen leaders gathered—farmers with calloused hands, healers with herb-stained fingers, outcasts with scars and defiance in their eyes. Elara stood before them, her heart pounding. She wasn't a hero, but she could be honest.

"I'm not from your world," she began, her voice carrying in the quiet. "I'm a farmer's daughter, a healer's apprentice. I know fear, doubt, the ache of leaving home. But I've seen Aurora's beauty—its rivers, its trees, its light. Morgath's stealing that from you, from us. We can stop her, but only if we fight together."

A grizzled farmer named Torv leaned forward, his voice rough. "Why should we trust a mortal? You'll run back to your world when things get hard."

Elara met his gaze, her empathy stirring. "I left my family to be here. I've faced Morgath's wraiths, her trials. I'm not running. I'm asking you to stand with me, for Aurora."

Kael's tail flicked, his grin approving. "She's got more spine than half of you lot."

A young healer, Lila, spoke up, her voice trembling but fierce. "I've lost friends to Morgath's curse. If there's a chance to save Liora, I'm in."

One by one, others nodded—Rhea, Torv, an outcast named Gavyn with a scarred face and a quiet resolve. Elara's chest swelled with hope, but a prickle of unease lingered. Gavyn's eyes darted too often, his hands fidgeting with a glowing stone. She pushed the thought aside—paranoia wouldn't help.

As night deepened, the camp buzzed with preparations. Elara helped distribute supplies, her hands steady as she bandaged a child's scraped knee, echoing her mother's lessons. Alaric trained fighters, his sword flashing in the twilight, while Kael scouted the perimeter, his cunning eyes scanning for wraiths.

But as Elara sat by a fire, the shard warm in her palm, Gavyn approached, his voice low. "You really think we can win?" he asked, his scarred face unreadable.

"I have to," Elara said, meeting his gaze. "For Aurora. For my home."

He nodded, but his eyes lingered on the shard, a flicker of something—greed, fear?—crossing his face. Before she could question him, Kael bounded over, his fur bristling. "Trouble," he hissed. "Wraiths, closing in."

Elara leapt to her feet, her dagger drawn. Alaric joined them, his sword gleaming, as Rhea rallied the camp. The twilight darkened, and a chorus of hisses slithered from the trees. Elara's heart sank as she saw Gavyn slip away, his form vanishing into the shadows.

"He's gone to Morgath," Kael growled, his claws unsheathed. "I smelled her magic on him."

Betrayal stung Elara's chest, but there was no time to dwell. Wraiths surged from the trees, their ember-eyes blazing. Alaric's sword flashed, Kael darted through the chaos, and Elara gripped the shard, its warmth urging her forward. The Dawnfields erupted into battle, and she knew their plan was compromised. Morgath was coming, and the fight for Aurora's soul had begun.

Chapter 14:

The Dawnbringer's Stand

The Dawnfields blazed with chaos as shadow-wraiths poured from the twilight, their ember-eyes cutting through the mist like malevolent stars. Elara stood at the heart of the battle, her dagger gripped tightly, the shard of the Heart of Radiance pulsing against her chest. Around her, Aurora's rebels—farmers, healers, outcasts—fought with makeshift weapons and raw determination, their shouts mingling with the wraiths' guttural hisses. The air crackled with Morgath's dark magic, but Elara's resolve burned brighter, fueled by the unity she'd forged and the prophecy she'd embraced.

Ser Alaric swung his sword beside her, his scarred armor dented but unyielding, cleaving through a wraith that lunged at a young healer. "Hold the line!" he roared, his voice a beacon in the fray. Kael darted through the chaos, his orange fur a blur as he tripped wraiths with cunning leaps, guiding children to safety behind glowing wards.

Elara's heart pounded, her eyes scanning for Morgath. Gavyn's betrayal had brought the sorceress's forces here, shattering their element of surprise, but the shard's warmth reminded her of Sylvara's words: ""Only through courage and unity shall the curse be broken."" The Heart's power wasn't in its crystal form—it was in Aurora's people, in their shared light. She had to reach them, channel their magic, before Morgath crushed them all.

"Rhea!" Elara shouted, spotting the healer leader amidst the battle, her staff glowing as she deflected a wraith's claws. "We need to unite the camp—now!"

Rhea nodded, her braided hair whipping as she called to her fighters. "To the center! Protect the dawnbringer!"

The rebels rallied, forming a tight circle around Elara, their faces etched with fear but lit with defiance. Torv, the grizzled farmer, wielded a pitchfork like a spear, while Lila, the young healer, chanted a spell that sent vines snaring wraiths. Elara climbed onto a crate, the shard raised high, its glow piercing the twilight.

"People of Aurora!" she cried, her voice carrying over the din. "Morgath wants us broken, alone. But we're stronger together. Your light—your courage, your hope—is the Heart of Radiance. Lend it to me, and we'll free Liora!"

The shard flared, its light spreading, touching each rebel. Their eyes widened as they felt it—a spark of Aurora's magic, dormant but alive. Hands linked, voices rose in a wordless chant, and the glow intensified, pushing back the wraiths' darkness.

But a cold laugh sliced through the harmony. Morgath materialized at the field's edge, her black robes swirling like a storm, her silver hair a cruel mockery of Liora's radiance. In her hand, she held the crystal orb imprisoning Liora's spirit, its light dimming under her grip. "Foolish dawnbringer," she sneered, her voice a blade of ice. "You think your rabble can challenge me?"

Elara's heart faltered, but she stood firm, the shard's warmth steadying her. "You're the one who's alone, Morgath. You stole Aurora's light, but you can't steal its heart."

Morgath's eyes blazed, and she raised her hand, dark energy crackling. "Then I'll crush it."

A wave of shadow surged toward the rebels, but Alaric leapt forward, his sword glowing with borrowed light from the shard. "For Liora!" he roared, slashing through the wave, his blade meeting Morgath's magic with a deafening clash.

Kael darted to Elara's side, his claws unsheathed. "Now, dawnbringer! Channel the light before she turns us into wraith chow!"

Elara closed her eyes, drawing on the lessons of her parents—her father's resilience, her mother's compassion. She reached out, not with her hands but with her heart, feeling the rebels' magic flow into her. Torv's stubborn strength, Lila's quiet hope, Rhea's fierce resolve—it wove together, a tapestry of light that pulsed through the shard.

The glow erupted, a radiant beam that struck the orb in Morgath's hand. The sorceress screamed, her magic faltering as cracks spiderwebbed across the orb. Liora's spirit flickered within, a silhouette of silver and starlight, straining to break free.

"You can't stop me!" Morgath snarled, her form growing larger, shadows coiling around her like serpents. She hurled a bolt of darkness at Elara, but Alaric stepped into its path, his sword raised. The blast struck him, and he fell, his armor smoking, his face contorted in pain.

"Alaric!" Elara cried, her voice breaking. She leapt from the crate, kneeling beside him. His breath was shallow, but his eyes met hers, fierce and unyielding.

"Finish it," he rasped. "For Aurora."

Kael snarled, launching himself at Morgath, his agility drawing her attention. "Hey, witch! Pick on someone your own size!"

Elara's tears fell, but she rose, the shard blazing in her hand. She poured everything into it—her fear, her love, her belief in Aurora's people. The rebels' chant grew louder, their light overwhelming the wraiths, who dissolved into smoke. The beam from the shard intensified, shattering the orb with a sound like breaking glass.

Liora's spirit surged free, a radiant figure of silver light. She raised her hands, and Aurora's magic flooded back—rivers glowing, trees humming, the twilight sky brightening to a dawn-like glow. Morgath screamed, her shadows unraveling as Liora's light burned through her.

"You're nothing!" Morgath spat, her form flickering. "A girl, a mortal—"

"I'm the dawnbringer," Elara said, her voice steady, echoing with the strength of her allies. She thrust the shard forward, its light merging with Liora's, striking Morgath's heart. The sorceress shattered, her scream fading into silence, her essence scattering like ash.

The battlefield stilled. The wraiths were gone, the rebels standing in awe as Liora's spirit solidified, her silver hair flowing, her eyes warm with gratitude. "Thank you, dawnbringer," she said, her voice a melody of light. "You've saved us all."

Elara's knees buckled, exhaustion crashing over her. Kael caught her, his grin weary but triumphant. "Not bad for a farmer's daughter."

She looked to Alaric, fear gripping her, but Rhea was already at his side, her healing magic glowing. "He'll live," the healer said, her voice soft. "Thanks to you."

The Dawnfields bloomed with light, the grass shimmering, the air humming with renewed magic. Liora raised her hands, and the sky brightened further, a true dawn breaking for the first time in centuries. The rebels cheered, their voices a chorus of hope, and Elara felt the shard's warmth fade, its purpose fulfilled.

But as she looked at Liora, a chill ran through her. Morgath's final words—""You're nothing""— carried a hint of something darker, a whisper of a threat not fully vanquished. She pushed it aside, focusing on the victory, on the faces of those she'd fought for.

"You're home, dawnbringer," Kael said, nudging her shoulder. "What now?"

Elara smiled, her heart full yet heavy. "I go back to Briarwood," she said. "But I'll carry Aurora with me."

As the rebels celebrated, Elara stood with Kael and Alaric, the dawn's light warming her face. The battle was won, but the shard's faint pulse in her palm whispered of future challenges, a promise that her role as dawnbringer was far from over.

Chapter 15:

Homeward Bound

The golden fields of Briarwood stretched before Elara, swaying gently under the midday sun, their familiar scent of earth and wheat wrapping around her like a warm embrace. She stood at the village's edge, her cloak tattered from Aurora's trials, the stone map tucked safely in her bag, its carvings now dormant but heavy with memory. The door to Aurora had closed behind her, its ancient oak vanishing into Brackenwood Forest, leaving only the rustle of leaves and a faint hum of magic she could still feel in her bones. She was home, yet she felt like a stranger in her own skin.

The dawnbringer. The title echoed in her mind, a mantle she'd earned through trials of whispers, shadows, and fire. She'd faced Morgath, freed Princess Liora, and rallied Aurora's people to restore their realm. The Heart of Radiance's shard, now cool and quiet in her pocket, was a reminder of that victory—and the cost. Alaric's scars, Kael's fierce loyalty, the rebels' courage—they were etched in her heart, alongside the ache of leaving them behind.

Elara adjusted her bag and stepped onto the dirt path leading to her family's cottage. The village was as she'd left it: thatched roofs gleaming in the sun, the blacksmith's hammer ringing, children laughing as they chased a stray goat. But everything felt different, as if Aurora's twilight had sharpened her senses. She noticed the worry lines on a farmer's face, the quiet strength in a mother's stride, the way the fields seemed to hum with life, echoing Aurora's rivers.

As she neared the cottage, the door swung open, and her mother, Mara, stood there, her silver-streaked braid catching the light. Her brown eyes widened, then filled with tears. "Elara!" she cried, rushing forward to envelop her in a fierce hug.

Elara buried her face in her mother's shoulder, the scent of herbs and home grounding her. "I'm sorry," she whispered, her voice breaking. "I didn't mean to worry you."

Her father, Thom, appeared behind them, his weathered face softening with relief. "You're back," he said, his voice thick as he pulled her into his arms. "That's all that matters."

They led her inside, the cottage's warmth wrapping around her—oak table, woven tapestries, the crackle of the hearth. Over a simple meal of stew and bread, Elara told her story, her words halting at first but gaining strength. She spoke of Brackenwood's dangers, the glowing map, Aurora's twilight skies, and the trials that tested her soul. She described Kael's cunning, Alaric's redemption, and the moment she stood against Morgath, the shard blazing with the rebels' light. Her parents listened, their faces a mix of awe, fear, and pride.

"You found the door," Thom said softly, his hazel eyes—mirrors of her own—glistening. "The one from my stories."

Elara nodded, pulling the shard from her pocket. Its faint glow flickered in the firelight, a relic of another world. "It was real, Papa. All of it."

Mara took her hand, her touch gentle but firm. "You've changed, Elara. You're not just our girl anymore."

The words stung, but Elara knew they were true. She was still their daughter, but she was also the dawnbringer, shaped by courage and loss. She thought of Alaric, rebuilding Aurora with Liora, and Kael, no doubt causing mischief in the Dawnfields. Would she ever see them again?

"I'm still me," she said, her voice soft but certain. "But I've seen what I can do, what people can do together. I want to help here, in Briarwood, the way I helped there."

Thom smiled, a quiet pride in his gaze. "Then you'll be a healer, a leader, whatever this village needs. You've always had that heart."

That evening, Elara walked to the fields, the sun dipping low, painting the sky in hues that reminded her of Aurora's twilight. She sat on a familiar log, the one where her father had first told her of the magical door. The shard rested in her palm, its glow faint but persistent, as if whispering of unfinished stories. Morgath was gone, but her final words—""You're nothing""—had carried a shadow, a hint of something lurking beyond the victory. Was Aurora truly safe, or would another threat rise?

A rustle in the grass made her tense, her hand reaching for the dagger she still carried. But it was only a fox, its fur a soft orange, its eyes glinting with mischief. It tilted its head, then darted into the forest, leaving Elara with a fleeting smile. "Kael, you trickster," she murmured, though she knew it couldn't be him. Or could it?

She stood, tucking the shard away, her gaze lingering on Brackenwood's dark silhouette. The door was gone, but Aurora felt close, a part of her now. She was Elara of Briarwood, healer's apprentice, farmer's daughter, dawnbringer. Whatever lay ahead—here or beyond—she was ready.

As she turned toward home, the wind carried a faint hum, like a distant river of light, calling her to new horizons.

Epilogue:

A Shadow Stirs

In the heart of Aurora, where the Dawnfields once burned with battle, a gentle dawn bathed the land in hues of gold and rose. The rivers of liquid light flowed freely again, their melodies weaving through the air, harmonizing with the rustle of newly vibrant trees. The twilight that had gripped the realm for centuries was gone, replaced by a cycle of day and night, a gift from Princess Liora's restored magic. Villagers from Lumina and the Dawnfields danced under the open sky, their laughter echoing as they rebuilt homes and replanted fields, their hearts alight with hope.

At the edge of the fields, Ser Alaric stood watch, his scarred armor polished but bearing the marks of his redemption. His gray eyes scanned the horizon, ever vigilant, though his posture was less rigid, softened by the peace he'd fought for. Beside him, Kael lounged on a glowing rock, his orange fur catching the sunlight, his tail flicking with restless mischief. "You ever gonna relax, old man?" Kael teased, his grin sharp. "Morgath's dust, and we've got a proper sunrise for once."

Alaric's lips twitched, a rare hint of a smile. "Peace is fragile, trickster. You'd do well to remember that."

Kael snorted, stretching lazily. "Let me enjoy the moment before you drag us into another fight. Besides, the dawnbringer's back in her world, probably plowing fields and boring herself to death."

Alaric's gaze softened at the mention of Elara. "She gave us this dawn. Wherever she is, she carries Aurora's light."

In the distance, Liora walked among her people, her silver hair shimmering, her presence a beacon of renewal. She paused to help a child plant a glowing seed, her laughter bright, but her eyes held a quiet weight. The Heart of Radiance was gone, its power woven into Aurora's soul, but its absence left a faint ache, a reminder of the cost of victory.

Yet, deep beneath the Dawnfields, where no light reached, something stirred. In a forgotten cavern, its walls cracked and pulsing with residual dark magic, a shard of Morgath's essence flickered—a wisp of shadow, formless but alive. It slithered across the stone, drawn to a pool of stagnant water where the sorceress's final spell had pooled, a remnant of her shattered will. The shadow whispered, its voice a hiss of malice: ""The dawnbringer thinks me vanquished, but darkness endures.""

The pool rippled, reflecting not the cavern but a glimpse of Briarwood—Elara walking through her fields, the shard of the Heart in her pocket, its glow faint but persistent. The shadow's hiss grew sharper, hungry. ""You will call me back, mortal. And I will rise.""

Above, the celebration continued, unaware of the stirring below. Liora glanced at the ground, a fleeting unease crossing her face, but she shook it off, turning back to her people. Kael's ears twitched, his grin faltering for a moment, but he dismissed it as the wind. Alaric's hand rested on his sword, his instincts prickling, though he saw no threat.

In Briarwood, Elara paused on her path, the shard warming against her side. She looked toward Brackenwood Forest, a shiver running through her. The door was gone, but the call of adventure lingered, a whisper of something unfinished. She smiled, tucking the shard away, and walked on, her heart steady but her senses alert.

The shadow beneath Aurora pulsed, biding its time, its whisper fading into the dark: ""Soon.""

END